A Punch To The Heart

short crime stories

Andrew Humphrey

All stories are original to this collection other than *Vinegar Lake* which appeared in *Crimeucopia* (Murderous-Ink Press) 2021

Cover art by Peter Corr
(www.petercorrart.com)

ISBN number: 978-1-7398195-6-9

Printed and Bound by 4Edge

Published by:

Head Shot
85 Gertrude Road
Norwich
UK

editorheadshot@gmail.com
www.headshotpress.com

A Punch To The Heart

Many thanks to Mario Guslandi for the use of the quote on the cover and to Peter Corr for his excellent photography.

And thank you, of course, to Andrew Hook, for his constant support and advice.

Contents

Anyway

I sat on the bed in a white hotel bathrobe pondering breakfast. Cereal *and* pastries *and* a full English? Probably, I thought, ignoring my thickening waistline, why not?

Julie was already dressed. She clipped earrings on, head tilting to one side then the other. "Are you going to sit there all day?"

"Quite possibly."

"We've got to be out by ten."

I lay back heavily. The bed was very soft and I sunk into it, my robe falling open.

"Put that away, Philip," Julie said mildly. "Jesus." She adjusted her lipstick a little, using the blank TV screen as a mirror.

I did as I was told. I tried to sit up. It was a struggle. The bed really was *very* soft. I managed eventually. "I'll have a shower then." I was little out of breath.

"Good." She patted her sides briskly, stood on tiptoe for a moment then eased her bare feet into black, heeled shoes. There was a full length mirror in the bathroom and she inspected herself, heels clattering on the tiled floor. She was immaculate, of course. Trim and lithe and unnecessarily pretty. She wore a caramel-coloured cardigan over a white blouse. Her skirt was dark and fitted perfectly across slender hips.

"Gorgeous. As ever." I placed a hand on her arm as I joined her in the bathroom. The cardigan was made of soft wool and I rubbed it gently.

She grunted and moved away, glancing at her watch. "I'm going to pop to reception, grab a paper. Something to read while you … ablute."

"Cool," I said, as though I was not, in fact, fifty-five years old.

She slipped past me. We didn't kiss. At the door she said, "Shall I take the key? Lock you in?"

"Nah. I'll take my chances. Give the cleaner a treat if she turns up early."

Julie sighed. She was halfway through the door. "Anyway," she said. The last I saw of her was her left hand. She gave her fingers a little waggle, the door closed and she was gone.

I took a long shower. I was a little hungover; I'd finished off a bottle of a rich red with dinner the previous evening. Julie was in training for a half-marathon. No alcohol for her. No dessert either. I closed my eyes and let the water hit my face. It was hot, a little too hot, perhaps, but it felt good, driving the sleep and graininess from my eyes. I emptied the tiny, complimentary bottle of Moulton Brown shower gel into my palm and sluiced it across my chest and belly. I considered a wank but I couldn't be bothered. I turned off the shower and dried myself quickly. I left my towels puddled on the bathroom floor. I knew that Julie would tidy them up before we left.

Naked, I stepped out of the bathroom. I was surprised that Julie had not yet returned as it was less than a minute's walk to reception. She could be chatting, I thought, but that wasn't really her style. I dressed in the clothes that I'd worn the night before. I pulled the thin cotton curtains across. The day was still and quiet. No sign of Julie. The room was silent. I was not entirely sure what to do.

DI Minto sits opposite me. I'm at the police station in Norwich. I'm not under arrest. Minto has been at pains to stress this. If this were a television program I would be shouting at him now, telling him to stop wasting time on me and to get out there and find my wife. I don't do this because, despite some evidence to the contrary, I am not an imbecile.

"Thank you for your time," he says again. He is polite and appears kind. He is my age, I suppose, perhaps a little younger. I find that I like him. As though that matters at all.

"It's been eighteen hours," I say. "Isn't that extraordinary?"

Minto says nothing. His hands are steepled in front of him. Ostensibly he is smartly dressed – white shirt, blue tie, navy suit – but he appears frayed at the edges, worn down, resigned.

Eighteen hours. It *is* extraordinary, but only because time no longer has any meaning. It could be ten seconds, ten years since I last saw Julie, for all I know or understand.

"It was your anniversary?"

"That was Saturday. Thirty one years. We always go to Brancaster. We spent our honeymoon there. All we could afford in those days."

"The North Norfolk coast? Not exactly cheap."

"It wasn't so trendy then. And it was only a long weekend in a B & B." I think of Julie, the day after our wedding, pulling me towards the beach. Her hair was longer then, tangled in sunlight. She wore a lemon dress with thin straps. Her legs were bare.

"You've stayed at that hotel before?"

"Several times. Not every year but more often than not."

"They know you there, I should imagine?"

"Some do. Not all. High staff turnover, casual workers and all that."

"How about the receptionist?"

"Mary?"

"You know her name?"

"She wears a label with her name on it, DI Minto. As I'm sure you know."

"Call me John. Please."

"John. Okay. Yes, we knew Mary. And she remembered us." A tiny prick of impatience stirs me. "I assume you have spoken to her?"

"Of course."

"And I have already given my account, at the hotel, to your DS. I appreciate it may have been a little garbled, but ..."

"This is what we do, Mr Avery. We take statements. We double check. It's tedious but it must be done."

"I understand." Do I? "And if you're John, I'm Phillip."

"Phillip," he says slowly. He has a pad in front of him and he peers down at it. His skin is sallow. He doesn't appear entirely well, but the lighting in this dull, metallic room is poor. It could be that. "Phillip," he says again, "I need to ask you some questions. Quite routine. You may find some offensive. But they must be asked. I'm sure you understand."

I nod gormlessly. "Ask away."

He does and I answer thus:

"Yes. We were … are happy. Mostly. Thirty one years. Nobody is perfect. What does one expect?"

"Arguments? Not exactly. Some silences, I suppose. Sulks. You know how women can be." He looks up at that, sharply. "Are you married, John?" I say.

I was, he says. I give a little grimace and he looks down at his pad again, asks another question.

"No, I don't know anyone who would harm Julie. She can be a little sharp, sometimes. Who can't? Doesn't suffer fools, as they say. But no. She *is* in HR, I suppose. Still. She is loved. I think. On balance."

"Affairs? No. Not on my part." Not for want of trying, I think.

And Julie, he says.

I falter and he sits up straight, pushing the pad to one side.

Take your time, Phillip.

"Yes. Julie did … see someone else for a while." Six words. Jesus.

I'll need the details. Names. Dates.

May as well run a blade across my balls, I think, but I smile and speak some words in a certain order. Each word a nail, each sentence a hammer. "But we're fine now," I say eventually. "Water under the bridge and all that."

He stops writing and looks at me.

There's knock on the door and a WPC enters. She's young, of Asian descent and she's extremely pretty. I notice these things. I notice myself noticing these things, even under these circumstances. I should hate myself but I don't.

She touches Minto's shoulder and says something quietly to him. I smile at her. She doesn't smile back. Minto says, "Will you excuse me for a moment, Mr Avery?"

*

The hotel is a large converted Victorian farmhouse. Our room was in an old stable block adjacent to the main building. It took forty eight seconds to cross the shingled courtyard that separated our room from reception. I smelled bacon as soon as I opened the main door. Where was Julie? I wanted my breakfast.

The desk was unattended. I approached it, peered round a corner. "Mary?" I said.

A woman appeared. Middle-aged, coltish, alert. White blouse, black skirt, a uniform of sorts, I supposed. She had a mass of hair, the colour of hazel and artfully arranged. Good calves, I noticed. Her smile as she approached me was uncertain but not unattractive.

"Have you seen my wife?"

"Your wife?" she said, her smile faltering further, threatening to slide off her face completely.

A couple appeared from another corridor before I could speak. The man was tall and broad, sporting a multi-coloured golfing top and a large, aggressive moustache. The woman was vinegar-thin, sour-faced, in a smock dress and immaculate jeans. The man pulled two suitcases behind him, the woman had a miniscule bag slung across her right shoulder. "Shop," he said, genial, dismissive. "Bill, please." He saw me, faced me square on and said, "Excellent breakfast. Black pudding. Kedgeree. The full works."

"Great," I said, avoiding eye contact and sidling off towards the smell of bacon.

He was right, the breakfast was excellent. It felt odd, I suppose, eating alone, the empty chair opposite, the table set, pristine, ignored. I thought of another breakfast, in this room, with its high ceilings and its genial morning bustle, twenty years earlier. Julie sat opposite me then, in a summery dress, a thin fabric, flowered print, her throat bare. Sun-warm skin, the scent of her. That was before James, of course. Before James.

Now I had a plate full of bacon and sausage and egg and black pudding. Limitless coffee. Toast and butter. Pastries and cereal. Fruit, as a last resort. I ate and ate. I didn't really want to stop.

Minto returns eventually, as does the WPC. They sit carefully. The WPC says in a neutral voice, "Would you like a solicitor, Mr Avery?"

Her eyes are a lovely liquid brown.

I look at Minto. "Do I need one?"

He pinches the bridge of his nose. He looks sad, disappointed. "You tell me."

The door has a frosted glass partition, as does the wall next to it. Shapes are moving, gathering beyond the glass.

I look at the wall to Minto's right. It's the colour of mud. There are scuff marks and some are high up on the wall, which seems curious.

"I don't suppose it matters much," I say.

You won, old boy, a friend said once, after our weekly squash game, still in our whites, at the bar, an orange juice each, condensation on the glasses.

Won? Not the squash. Never the squash. James. He was talking about James. Or rather I had been talking about him. Again.

Won?

Well, he's gone, hasn't he? She chose you.

Won?

I wanted to pull him to me, to pepper his face with my spittle. I wanted to say, won? I won? When I kiss her – when she lets me kiss her – I taste him. On her lips, on her skin. I wanted to say this but I didn't. I sipped my drink and we fixed the date for our next game.

"We need to go through it all again, Mr Avery."

"We do?"

"I think you know we do. From Friday, when you booked into the hotel."

"When *we* booked into the hotel." Minto looks at the WPC who looks at me and then away again. "Do you have a name?" I say to her.

"Patel," she says, surprised into it, broadsided a little.

"Patel," I say. Disappointing. Banal. Stereotypical, even. Or perhaps I'm the stereotype, the cuckold, frozen in one time, one place whilst everything and everyone moves past me soundless, effortless, indifferent.

"You were alone, Mr Avery. The booking was made for you both but nobody at the hotel has any recollection of seeing Mrs Avery at all."

"That's ridiculous. We had dinner together."

"You had dinner alone." He looks down then up again. His eyes are softer, pitying. "You were talking to yourself all evening. And again at breakfast. That's why Mary … Mrs Walker … called us. She was worried about you."

I feel myself frown. I am wearing the same short-sleeved shirt as the day before. Julie has washed this shirt, ironed it. Her DNA is on it, I expect. Is her DNA on me, I wonder? And mine on her? After all these years it should be, it should be ingrained, buried deep. But I wonder. Goose pimples form on my bare arms and I run a hand across them.

After breakfast I walked to the car. I'm not sure what I expected. Would Julie be sitting there, in the passenger seat, seatbelt on, arms crossed, waiting? Of course not.

It had been cool so far, this fledgling summer. Damp. Today was dry, at least, the clouds high and thin enough to barely matter.

I ran a hand across the roof of the car. I opened the passenger door then closed it again. I checked in the boot, although for what I was not entirely sure.

The coast road runs past the hotel's entrance. Look beyond it and fields slope down to marshland, then the beach, then the North Sea. There are walks here, many walks, most of which we have taken over the years, past reedbeds, saltmarsh, freshwater lagoons. That's where Julie is, I thought, despite the unpractical footwear. It's dry enough and the walking is easy.

That's where she is, I thought. Walking. Walking and thinking. Walking and thinking of him. Who else? Me? Hardly. Not now. Not anymore.

So I waited. I stood by the car and I waited for Julie.

"The thing is," Minto says, "we've spoken to your neighbours." He is speaking very carefully now, the words slow and deliberate, as though I'm a child. "They have seen no sign of your wife for ten days."

"My neighbours?"

"Mrs Lehane at number 32. Nice lady. Housebound. She says she waved to Mrs Avery most mornings as she left for work. She often saw her when she returned home too, six thirty on the dot. But nothing for the last ten days. Mrs Avery's car is still in the drive. She's hardly seen you either, as it happens."

"I work from home. Accountant. Chartered. Raking it in." Why did I say that? Who was I trying to impress? Patel? A final reflex? Life in the old dog yet?

"Where is your wife, Mr Avery?"

"She's been off sick."

He consults his notes. "Her office say that you texted them on the 22nd of May to let them know that your wife had a migraine. This was irregular but Mrs Avery has an excellent record and reputation at the firm so they let the five statutory sick days pass without comment. Since last Tuesday they have been trying to contact your wife; texts, emails, telephone calls. They've tried calling you too. On Friday they sent someone to your house. We received a call from the head of HR about an hour after Mary Walker contacted us." His head comes up again. "Where is your wife, Mr Avery?"

The air changes as he speaks, the light too. There are shadows where there were none. Patel holds her fingers against her brow. Her eyes are cast down.

Julie is memories, fragments. A calf, eyes, light through hair. How do they stand – glimpses, glances, the trace of a smile – against years and years, the solid, immutable shove of time? What did she really see all those years ago? An ordinary man, well set up. His own boss, comfortable already, better to come. I was leaner then but nothing special. A good bet, I suppose. A good solid bet.

"Mr Avery?" Minto says.

The door opens. Shadows gather. A telephone rings.

I feel my mind skittering off. I try to pull it back but it's having none of it.

Bad Milk

"I interviewed him once," Stella said. She takes a pull on her cigarette. I'm sad that she's smoking again. Not that it's any of my business. Not anymore. Not ever, really.

"I remember." Of course I remember. Stella ignores me. Sometimes it's reassuring how little things change.

"It's hard to see past the clichés; force of nature, all that guff." She taps ash into a plastic cup. The glass of white wine is untouched in front of her which is unusual in itself. "But he did...erupt into a room, you know? Heads turned. Grown men and women recalibrating, reassessing their position in the order of things. When he left it was a mess. Testosterone everywhere."

"You sound impressed."

"It was hard not to be. As you well know, Steven."

"I hated the bastard. As you well know, Stella."

She gives a tiny shrug as she stubs out the cigarette. Now she turns to the wine and two thirds of it disappears in a single swallow. That's more like it. "You know, he said at the end of the interview, I do like to leave behind a line of wet knickers and limp dicks."

"Classy."

"He made it sound funny. And he had that smile. Like a wolf. A nice wolf."

"Not so nice. Sounds like it was an invitation."

"Of course it was an invitation. You knew the man."

"Did you take him up on it?"

"I was with you at the time, Steven."

"And?"

She drains the wine. "Bastard," she says without heat.

Stella leaves and I have about thirty seconds to myself, which is lovely, but then mother is there. Of course she is. I'm in one of the drawing rooms. An obscure one. But that wasn't going to stop her.

"Here you are."

"Apparently."

Her dress is black, of course. It's buttoned down tightly, as is she. She's holding a crystal tumbler. It's almost empty. This is good. She'll need a refill in a minute.

"Which one was that?"

"Stella."

"Stella?"

"The journalist. Well, she used to be ..."

"Ah. Yes. The hack. She's with that American now, isn't she? Very handsome. Incredibly white teeth. He's something in money, isn't he?"

"We're all something in money, mother."

"Well, if you put it like that." She sat next to me. I inched away from her. It was a reflex. "Look, Steven. This won't do. Come and join the rest of us. People are asking questions."

"I shouldn't be here at all. Bloody hypocritical."

"No one cares about that." She examines her glass, which seems to have emptied itself without her consent. She appears disconcerted for a moment but soon rallies. "It's how it looks. That's what matters."

"Of course it is."

"It's bad enough that you wouldn't do the eulogy, you can at least make an appearance now. Say a few words."

"You wouldn't want to hear what I have to say, mother."

She tries to cry but it's so utterly unnatural it doesn't take at all. "Your poor brother."

"Don't give me that."

She produces a tissue from somewhere and dabs at her dry eyes. "Poor Seb. What would he say? What would he think?"

"He'd love the attention."

She stands, examining her glass again. "You were spoilt. I blame your father." That's a good one, but I let it go. "I'll give you five minutes, Steven, then you're out of the will."

She leaves the room with a dignified flounce. I'm alone again and it's great.

I go for a walk in the grounds before anyone else can collar me. It's early evening and the light is draining from a clear sky. It's spring. The air is soft and warm. It's been a good day to bury one's only brother.

There's a fine view of the house from the croquet lawn. It looks magnificent, from a distance. Old brick, clean lines, many windows, some turrets. It exudes an air of money and privilege. It's only when you get closer that the cracks appear. And you can say that about anything, can't you? Anyone. I know that the National Trust have been sniffing around. Mother's given them pretty short shrift. At least she says she has. Can't have the plebs trolling around. Still, I wonder sometimes.

I'm by the entrance to the maze, considering whether to have a trot round, for old time's sake, when

I see Emma. There's a retaining wall across from the maze, it backs onto a curved, sweeping expanse of lawn. Emma is sitting on it. She makes a good widow. I always thought she would. Her black dress is sleek and demure. And sexy as hell. I probably won't mention that. Not really the time.

She sees me and nods at a space on the wall next to her. I join her. Sit.

"Emma."

"Steven."

"Do you have a cigarette?"

"I don't smoke."

"Of course you don't."

"Neither do you."

"Well. First day of the rest of my life now, isn't it? Anything goes."

"I think you can do a little better than taking up smoking, Emma."

"That's so sweet." Her bare arms are braced against the wall. She leans into me a little. She smells fantastic. "Isn't that sweet?" she says again, as though there's someone else there.

I suddenly have no idea what to say. The words that come are, "I suppose you'll get the house?"

She gives me a look. "I should bloody well hope so. All of them, actually. I put the years in after all."

"Of course. I didn't mean …"

"Oh, stop it, Steven. I know you can't say you're sorry."

"I'm not sorry."

"Kind of my point."

"Are you?"

She pauses at that, stands, brushes dust from her backside. "We were married for fifteen years. He is the father of my children."

"Where are the children?"

"At school. No need to interrupt their education for this."

"No."

"So … sorry. I'm not sure that's the word. The thing is, Steven, he could be such a cunt." I look at her. "Oh, come on. I'm sure you're familiar with the word."

"Of course. It was just the way you said it. Seb used to think it was my name. Mind you, the last time he called me it I was trying to blackmail him so it was fair enough, I suppose."

"The photos?" I nod. "What were you thinking? He didn't care. Everyone knew he screwed around."

"I had to try something."

"Why? It couldn't have been for money."

"He didn't tell you?"

"He just laughed at you, Steven. He liked the pictures. He thought they got his good side."

"He was in the cabinet, Emma."

"So? He wasn't the worst Foreign Secretary."

"Actually, Emma, he was. Against some pretty stiff opposition. But he wouldn't have stopped there, would he?"

"Of course not. I used to hear him, in the bathroom, practising his speeches. And PMQ's. He'd do all the voices. Ask himself questions, answer them as though he was the PM. He was good, actually."

"He was quite an orator. I'll give him that. It was what he said that was the problem." I stand and stretch. I want a drink. "I told him to resign. From the cabinet. From the Party. Or I'd give the pictures to Stella."

"And you would have?"

"Yes. But he beat me to it. Through a friendly hack."

"Yes. I do remember that."

"Nobody gave a shit."

"*I* gave a shit, Steven."

"Of course. Sorry."

She sighs and her head tilts back. "Well, not that much of a shit, if I'm honest. Nothing I didn't know and all that."

"Still."

"Yes. Still." She gathers herself. "I always liked Stella. We chatted a little earlier. She's different to your others. I'm not sure what it is."

"She's quite intelligent, I suppose."

"Yes, that's probably it. Where's the current one? Steph, is it?"

"She's at home. At *her* home. She doesn't know about this."

"Doesn't know about it? Doesn't she watch the news, read the papers?"

"Well, no actually. She's quite young. Not indecently so, I must stress."

"Of course not. By the tone of your voice I gather that she's wearing a bit thin?"

"A little."

"Got the next one lined up? Your relationships always seemed to *overlap* a little as I recall."

The cheek of it. I think of Seb's conquests, not so much overlapping as stacked one atop the other like a vertiginous, fleshy tower. "It's you, of course, Emma. It's always been you."

She bristles a little. "Don't take the piss."

"What? Too soon?"

"Perhaps a little. All things considered." She steps away from the wall and brushes herself down again, although her dress appears completely clean. "We should go in."

"Do we have to?"

"I think we do. We'll be missed."

"After you."

"We'll go together." She links her arm in mine, which surprises me. We walk side by side through the fragrant air.

As it happens Seb killed his own political ambitions without any outside help or interference. It was a party do, at his London home. One of the waiters was black. Seb made a comment referencing this. Then another and another. One of staff managed to record most of the exchange and sold it to the papers the following day. And that was that. The odd thing is, I don't think Seb was a racist. Not particularly. I honestly don't know what he was thinking. But then I rarely did.

He went back into business. The family business. Money. We're generations deep in the stuff. We were handling futures and hedge funds before anyone knew what they were. Cash breeds. It blooms and blossoms. It has a life of its own. All we did was marshal it, shepherd it into nooks and crannies, away from the light, away from where it could do anyone but us any good. Now we subcontract to bright young things and when they burn out we get some more. Officially I'm a hedge fund manager. I have an office in the City which I attend from time to time. I chair meetings occasionally and sometimes I even listen to what is said. Seb's life was much the same but with added politics and a need for power. He had charisma, mother said. Well, not just her, to be fair. Character. Actually, all he had was ego. I almost admired the limitless extent of it. Almost. His ego bred a monstrous self-confidence and a dark, malleable, testosterone-driven charm that consumed all in his path. Except me.

*

When we reach the house the wake has broken down into a number of small, desultory clusters, scattered around drawing rooms, ante-chambers, libraries. Most of the major luminaries have gone, as have the press and the TV. The lights are low as darkness falls. Staff still circulate with trays of whisky and brandy and port.

Mother's in an ante-chamber, sitting next to an immaculate, grey-haired gentleman. Their knees are almost touching as they talk. When she sees us she stands quickly. The man does too, melting away with a bow.

"Steven. Emma."

"Mother," we say simultaneously.

"Long day," she says to Emma, laying a dry hand on her arm.

"Too long," Emma says.

"You'll stay?"

"No. Thank you."

Mother nods. Emma brushes my cheek with cold lips then leaves.

"You've let us all down," my mother says to me.

"So it's not been a complete waste."

"I assume you think you're being funny." I say nothing and we stand opposite each other like the complete strangers that we are. "Will you stay?"

"No."

"Of course not. Who's the lucky girl?"

"Steph."

"Do I know her?"

"No." Do *I* know her? Doubtful. To be fair, with Steph, there isn't a great deal to know.

"So be it." She sighs and then she hugs me, which is unexpected and horrible.

*

I'm not sure why Seb hated me. He was taller than me, better looking; more athletic … you get the picture. Not by much, just a stray gene or two. But that it's all it takes. And he was always mother's favourite and probably father's too, although it's hard to tell with someone who was only ever really a cipher, an absence, a father-shaped hole. Not jealousy then, I think we can rule that out.

During our earliest years we treated each other with a mostly benign indifference. There was no love, of course, no affection. Let's not be silly. But there was a kind of colourless neutrality that seemed to suit us both.

Then, when I was fifteen and he was thirteen, we entered the dining room together for breakfast. It was the summer holidays. We were briefly alone.

"Morning, cunt," he said.

"What?"

"You heard. Cunt."

"You can't speak to me like that."

He mimicked the words back at me in a childlike voice. He had already outgrown me. He had the build of a twenty year old, his shoulders broad beneath the white tennis shirt, forearms corded with fledgling muscle.

"What the hell has got into you, Seb?"

"You disgust me, that's all." His voice had become casual, almost conversational. He brushed a strand of straw-blond hair from his eyes. His cheeks were pink and smooth, his eyes blue and empty and guileless.

"I just don't …"

He crossed the room in two paces and slapped my cheek. It was the shock rather than pain that prompted the tears.

"Pathetic," he said, moving away from me, grabbing a plate and loading it with egg and toast and over-cooked bacon. He sat and started to eat. Without looking at me he said, "Say anything and I'll tell them that you let Jenkins suck you off."

Jenkins was one of the drivers. He had a taste for young boys but he was good at his job and Seb and I were probably too old for him now so the family kept it quiet.

Then mother came in with a couple of staff trailing behind her. "My word, aren't you two keen this morning. Steven? What on earth is wrong with you?"

"Stomach bug," Seb said. "He should probably go back to bed for a bit."

"Steven?" I nodded. "Go on then. You need to speak up for yourself, you know. Seb won't always be around to look out for you."

I stumbled up the stairs, cheek burning, eyes wet. I passed a maid, I don't remember her name. I was pretty sure that she smirked. I had her dismissed for an imaginary offence three weeks later.

Mother finds a car and a driver from somewhere. The man is familiar in an odd sort of way, in his pale grey suit and crisp white shirt. As he opens the rear door of the Lexus for me I tell him my destination. He nods then slides into the driver's seat. There's a thick sheet of Perspex between us so we don't have to speak. Not that I would have. There are ghosts of old acne scars at the base of the driver's neck and, although his hair is cut brutally short, a sprinkling of dandruff decorates the collar of his jacket.

Standards, I think. I'll have a word with someone. Then I remember him. He's one of Seb's men. Security. He probably served under Seb in Afghanistan, most of his security guys had. They loved him, Seb said, endlessly; would have followed him to the ends of the earth. Not that anyone ever contradicted him. Who would dare?

It's late by the time I get to Steph's and she's so wasted she can hardly speak. Not that it matters. I'm not there for the conversation.

Seb and I attended the same boarding school for a while and he, along with a small coterie of loyal, like-minded sociopaths, made my life an unremitting misery. The beatings became drearily, mindlessly routine. Seb wasn't always involved, happy to subcontract the physical purgatory of my existence to a couple of almost wordless, if enthusiastic, thugs.

Seb lost his virginity before I did. Of course he did. I started young as well, though, and had the sort of success with the opposite sex that one would expect of someone moderately attractive and extravagantly rich. But whoever I liked, whoever I flirted with or kissed or fingered or fucked, Seb would be there also, days later, sometimes hours, leering in my face making sure that I knew that he had been there too.

I made the mistake of becoming almost serious about one girl; she was from a nearby comprehensive so it would never have worked, but I harboured a ludicrous fantasy that it might for a while. She was called Maddie and she was small and pretty and breathtakingly open-minded. Perhaps I thought that Seb wouldn't lower himself and after three weeks I wondered if I was right but then he cornered me in the quad just before evening prayers.

He had Fletcher and Harding with him and they held me while he pushed his hand into my face. "Breath it in, Stevie-boy. Suck up that Maddie-smell." I made the mistake of opening my mouth and he slid his fingers in. I should have bitten him, I know, but, of course, I didn't. "Tastes good, but I guess you know that, huh? Thanks for breaking her in for me. Cunt."

Later I went to see the head boy. He's a cabinet minister now. I told him everything. He said that I was an embarrassment and that I should never speak to him again.

Two days after my brother's funeral I meet Stella in a coffee shop off Oxford Street.

"Not your usual haunt," I say, noting the sticky table top and the weak latte served in a tall, narrow, fluted glass.

"Fancied a change," Stella says.

"Sounds familiar."

"Steven," she sighs. "We don't need to score points anymore."

"Sorry. How's Brad?"

"Away. Business. You know."

I nod. She's not dressed to kill exactly but she's looking good in a burgundy trouser-suit and with her hair pulled back. "To what do I owe the honour?"

She sees something in my face. "Not *that*, Steven. Honestly."

"Am I that transparent?"

"Yes. You always were. Can't we just have a catch up? Old times' sake?"

I sip the Americano that I ordered in Brad's honour. It's appalling. "Of course. But it's more than that. I can read you too, Stella, remember?"

She pushes the latte away. It catches on the table top and caramel-coloured milk slops into the chipped saucer. "I heard a whisper. About Seb. He was over the limit. A *long* way over."

I run a finger along the rim of my coffee cup. "Two things. One; you are no longer a journalist. Two; that is barely credible. It would have come out by now, and anyway the one thing you could say for Seb was that he never had a drink when he was driving. And he loved driving, loved making an entrance in that stupid little sports car."

"Old habits, that's all."

"Who was doing the whispering?"

"I can't say."

"You don't need to worry about protecting sources, Stella. You're not …"

"Not a journalist. I know. But one gets so bored." She screws her face up a little and I get the sudden feeling that she's playing with me. "And, would it have come out? Bigger things have been covered up than an ex-foreign secretary drinking and driving. He only killed *himself*, after all."

"I was there. He was on Red Bull the entire evening."

"Yes. You were there. Why *were* you there, Steven? You've spent the last twenty years studiously avoiding your brother's company. But not on this particular evening. There are even photos. Previously the only pictures of you two together as adults were at your father's funeral."

"Charity do. Good causes. Couldn't be helped."

She puts both hands on the table and her head dips a little. Her eyes meet mine and I can see that she knows.

I left school before Seb which was a merciful release. I half-expected him to attend the same university as me but he chose St Andrews and then Sandhurst, followed by a stint in Afghanistan where he was decorated, obviously, and by all accounts, but mostly his, he saved lives and, quite possibly, secured the future of Western civilisation.

After the army he joined the party and was helicoptered into a safe Tory seat in the Home Counties – is there any other? – and thus became an MP with minimal effort on his part.

As adults our paths rarely crossed; the odd family thing, the occasional Christmas. These mostly passed without incident, apart from one New Year's Eve, when I awoke at four to find Seb's face leering over me. He had his hands around my throat. His breath stank of port and cigars. His mouth was open in a rictus grin and a single strand of his saliva dripped onto my lips. I tried to scream and couldn't. He released me and sat up. When he said, "Happy New Year, cunt," his voice was almost jocular, almost warm. In the morning I wondered if I had dreamt it, but when I saw Seb's face at breakfast I knew that I hadn't.

Mother bemoaned her sons' mutual estrangement to anyone who would listen. So mostly me, then. It was my fault, of course. I'd always been jealous and so on and so on. I let her rant. I had my inheritance to think about.

When Father had the decency to make himself permanently absent a couple of years ago by perishing in a skiing accident I could hardly avoid attending the funeral. Seb and I were pall-bearers. There's a photograph of us shaking hands. I remember the warmth of his flesh and the transistor-like hum and crackle of his personality, the radioactive glow of him, as all the moths gathered around his poisonous flame. I became a non-person as his hand dropped from mine. He hadn't even looked at me.

That was the last time I saw him before the party fundraiser that was to be the last social event of his life. He barely looked at me then, either, although he must have surprised that I was there. No matter. I saw him.

Emma sits on the edge of my bed, her back to me. She's fastening her bra in that expert way that women have. As she pulls the straps over her shoulders she says, "That was nice."

"Nice," I say. "Thanks."

"Don't be like that." She doesn't look at me. She does something with her hair then locates her blouse. She buttons it methodically.

"Like what?"

She turns towards me now. Her blouse is not fully buttoned and I can see her bra, which is the colour of ivory and is lacy and pretty and, one would imagine, expensive. I try to make the most of it as I'm pretty sure I won't be seeing it again. "Grow up, Steven." She's smiling and her voice is mild but the words sting all the same. "This was necessary. And it was coming, so to speak."

"But that's it?"

"Of course that's it. What did you expect?"

That's a good question. "More than this."

"Really?" She stands, tucks her blouse into her skirt and smooths herself down. She's instantly immaculate. "Let's face it, you just wanted to go where Seb had been."

The truth of that hits home and I hurl the sheets aside, locating boxer shorts and a t-shirt in an attempt to preserve what remains of my dignity. "That's ridiculous, Emma. Take it back."

"Take it back? Are we still at school?"

For a moment I wonder. "The earth didn't move, you know." I'm surprised by my petulance and a little disappointed.

"Nor for me, darling. Nor for me. But then it rarely does so I wouldn't feel too bad about that." She breezes past me. "I have to be somewhere."

"Of course."

"Oh, Stella keeps calling me. Wants to meet up. Any idea what that's all about?"

"None at all."

"Should be fun. We can exchange notes."

"That's not funny, Emma."

"No. Of course it isn't."

After she's gone I go back into the bedroom. Emma's scent is there, of course, and for a moment I think that Seb's is too.

I didn't mean to kill him. Humiliation was the aim. I thought he might have a prang in his silly little sports car but that was all. I imagined the fun the red tops would have with it, the sainted Sebastian Sallow being done for drunk driving. I hadn't thought that the family would cover it up. Would they if he hadn't died? Probably, I suppose.

It was easy, spiking his drinks. He virtually ran on Red Bull, drank gallons of the stuff. It never affected him, he said, which was another boast in a life that was full of them. He just liked the taste, apparently, which was rubbish because I tried it once and it was disgusting. It made me light-headed too, just a single can. But I've never had much tolerance for caffeine, not like Seb, whose constitution was so much more robust than mine, than anyone's.

The good thing about Red Bull is that it disguises

the taste of vodka. It was easy, keeping his glass topped up with the stuff, little and often. No one noticed or suspected; all the attention was on the man himself – the force of nature, pressing the flesh, flirting and cajoling – not his glass left on a mantelpiece or a table. Even his security seemed complacent, distracted. But what was there to see, to worry about?

Seb acknowledged me once, guiding me into a quiet corner, underneath a portrait of a distant uncle.

"This is a surprise, Steven." His hand was on my shoulder, amiable enough to anyone watching, but with his fingers digging in. "To what do we owe the pleasure?"

"Just doing my bit. For the party. You know."

"No more photos, I trust? No more little blackmailing games?"

"I'm past all that, Seb. I trust that you are too."

He bent towards me and I smelt his breath, saw the sweat that darkened his blond, floppy fringe. "You're bad milk, old boy. Cream gone over. You're a waste of good DNA." Then he pulled back, suddenly all bonhomie and charisma. He slapped my arm and my flesh tingled. "Come on, big brother, join the party. Have a drink or something. And for God's sake, put your hand in your pocket."

Others joined us and I slipped away.

He left early to almost everyone's dismay. "Things to see, people to do," he bellowed, an arm aloft, cheeks aflame. Did he not know? Did he not feel the alcohol surging through his system? He was always so drunk on himself, perhaps he didn't.

He never made it out of the drive. It's a long drive, admittedly, but still. He lost control on a shallow bend and drove straight into an oak. I doubt the tree, which is over six hundred years old, felt a thing. But

Seb did. No seatbelt. Straight through the windscreen. Game over.

I didn't mean to kill him. It was just a wonderful bonus.

In early June I'm summoned by mother. It's a chore but it can't be helped. I need to step up, she says. Now that Seb has gone. I can't be expected to fill his shoes, of course. Who could? But … but what? She never specifies.

Instead I endure an excruciating, endless lunch. Emma is there, which doesn't help. She looks exquisite but she barely speaks and doesn't once meet my eyes.

As the dessert things are being cleared away, mother says, "Will she be a problem? Stella?"

I realise she's speaking to Emma and that it's a continuation of an earlier conversation that did not include me.

Emma shakes her head. "We've paid her off."

"But she's rich anyway."

"The *American* is rich," Emma says. "Someone like Stella, they always want more."

"What is this?" I say.

"You mean you don't know?" my mother says. Her gaze is blurred and soft from the lunchtime wine but it still penetrates.

"No."

Emma stares at her hands and says nothing.

Mother says, "Is there anything you'd like to add, Steven? Anything at all?"

"Of course not. Why would there be?" I'm offered coffee but I reject it curtly. The curious silence stretches on and I say, "Anyway. I must go."

The relief is almost palpable. Mother makes a gesture and dandruff man appears, in the same grey suit, the same white shirt. I follow him into the hallway and out into the warm, dull air.

I give him Steph's address and he nods. I finished with Steph three weeks ago but there's a good chance that's she's forgotten all about that. Anyway, I'm not sure where else to go.

I seal myself into the back of the car and settle back. The base of the driver's neck is the colour of brick, the old scars ridged and ugly. His hair is razored close to the scalp.

I doze a little as we hit the M25. We sail past the usual junction but I assume the driver has thought of a better way. Then we pass another junction and I press the intercom and ask him what the hell he thinks he's doing. He says nothing.

The junction that we do take leads towards countryside and thick woods. We're travelling at sixty but I try the door anyway. It's locked. I reach for the phone in my jacket pocket but it's gone. The driver's neck is a deep angry red now and his scalp is awash with sweat. I try the door again, swallowing the acid that floods my throat.

Arthur

It was hours before we realised he was dead. Brenda and I were getting ready to close up. I thought he was asleep, we both did. This was not unreasonable. Arthur was often to be found slumped on the red leather sofa that sat next to the library's exit. The pose was familiar also; head thrown back, mouth wide open, dentures slightly askew.

"Your turn," I said.

Brenda was tidying chairs away, straightening things, restoring order. "What?"

"To wake Arthur."

"You're nearer. You do it. I'm busy." She fussed unnecessarily over a computer desk.

"Your turn. Anyway, he likes you best."

She sighed and shuffled past a trolley full of teenage fiction. Her body was soft-edged, over-sized, her face milky and bovine. There was a large plant next to the sofa. It was as tall as a man. Its drab green leaves had grown and spread covertly so that they overlapped the sofa, edging towards it as though considering a quiet coup. Arthur's right arm was splayed towards the plant, his head lolling towards his shoulder. His forefinger lay gently against the serrated edge of one of the leaves. It was as though they were communicating, exchanging secrets.

"Come on, mate," Brenda said. "Last orders. You know the score."

She didn't get too close. She certainly didn't want to touch him. Arthur stank. Not his fault, but there it was. It was an astonishing punch of a scent that accompanied Arthur like some vile twin. It was odd because Arthur's appearance was neat, tidy. He was always clean-shaven and although he wore the same clothes every day – grey cardigan, checked shirt, black polyester trousers – they seemed pressed, well cared for. As did he, somehow, despite the stench.

Brenda leant forward as she spoke, then stood abruptly. "Rob?"

"What?" I was leafing idly through a paperback. James Salter's *Light Years*. I'd read it twice already and would read it again.

"I don't think he's sleeping."

The police came, along with an ambulance. The constable who spoke to us was painfully young. He had a long, unblemished face and coy eyes that blinked slowly beneath long lashes. His voice was soft, reticent. I wondered if he was in the right job, how long he would last. Behind him two green-clad men manoeuvred Arthur onto a stretcher.

"He's not stiff yet," I heard one of them say. "Small mercies."

The policeman's radio crackled and he spoke into it. Curt, coded, meaningless to Brenda and I. Then he turned his doe eyes to us and said we could be getting away if we wanted.

"We need to lock up," Brenda said.

"Give us ten, fifteen minutes."

We waited outside. The pavement was still warm from the day's heat although the air was cooling as the light leached away.

"Shame we don't smoke," I said.

"What?"

"Be the ideal time, wouldn't it? Standing out here, waiting."

"I've never smoked."

"I tried one when I was fourteen. Made me sick. I thought it would help me fit in with the cool kids. It just made things worse."

"I thought you would have been one of the cool kids, Rob."

"Where on earth do you get that idea from?" Her soft, kind eyes flinched a little at that. "But thanks, though. I think."

She shrugged, grunted.

I pulled at the ID card that hung around my neck, stretching the lanyard, tilting it so I could see the awful photo of a seven years younger me. More hair, fewer lines, tighter flesh. "God, I feel ancient."

"You are quite old."

"Jesus. I'm barely forty."

"Well, from my perspective..." She smiled gently.

"Still," I said, glancing at the police car, the ambulance. "I was glad when the adults got here."

"I know what you mean."

"I say adults, that kid in there looks about twelve."

"Cute though."

"I thought I saw you looking."

"Are you saying that you didn't?"

"Not my type, sweetheart. Not my type at all."

"And what is your type, Rob?"

"I'm still working on it."

The stretcher bearers barrelled through the library door and we stepped aside. Brenda folded her meaty arms across her chest. She shivered a little. "How old do you think he was?"

"He was seventy eight," I said. "It was his birthday last Thursday."

Her head turned quickly towards mine. I said nothing. As one of the stretcher bearers opened the back door of the ambulance the other said, "One thing's for sure, he won't be getting any older."

We worked in a small branch of the Norfolk and Norwich Library. It was set on a side street on one of the several arterial roads that led out of the city.

Five of us worked there: Steve, the manager, Brenda and I, Toni and Jeremy, the youngest of us, more fresh-faced than even the mildly dreamy constable. We were not busy. Not ever. It was a quiet miracle that we were still open at all, what with the cuts that savaged any spending that the local authority considered non-essential. Steve thought that perhaps we were so tucked away, so utterly nondescript, that we had been forgotten about. Whatever the reason, we were grateful, all of us. It was as undemanding a job as could be imagined.

Someone dying in the library was out of the ordinary, a big deal. Consequently Steve gathered the five of us together early on Friday morning, hours before opening.

I got there first, then Brenda, then Steve.

"Have you two actually been home?" Steve said, with a kind of grin. Brenda started crying. "Shit. Sorry. It was just a joke. Not a good one, mind…"

"It's not that," Brenda said, knuckling her eyes, leaving them redder than ever. "I've never seen a dead body before. Not a real one. Loads on the telly, of course. Sorry, I was fine last night. Wasn't I, Rob?"

"Delayed reaction," I said. "Quite understandable, nothing to apologise for."

Steve patted Brenda's shoulder awkwardly. "Absolutely. It was a shock. Look, take the day off. A couple of days. We'll manage."

"I'll be fine," Brenda said.

"Really?" Steve said. He glanced at me. He looked wretched. Steve was not comfortable with emotions. He badly wanted Brenda to go home.

"It'll just be mum and Jeremy Kyle," Brenda said. "I'd rather be here with you lot."

"Thanks," I said.

She punched my arm but she was smiling at least.

When Toni and Jeremy turned up Steve clapped his hands together and said, "Gather round, guys."

He placed his hands on his hips and spread his legs slightly. I think it's what's called a power pose. He'd probably seen a Tory MP do it. Toni, standing next to me, smelling of her morning cigarette, mimicked the stance. Jeremy said, "Fuck's sake," under his breath and stifled a laugh. And that was that as far as Steve's authority was concerned.

"Come on, guys," he said, gamely. "This is serious."

"Stinky guy's dead," Toni said. "We'll burn the sofa and carry on as usual."

She had a way of cutting to the chase, did Toni.

Steve clapped his hands again. No one took any notice. Toni and Jeremy made their way to the kitchen for coffee and Brenda folded her arms and stared into the middle distance. "Bloody hell, guys. Really?"

"Give it up, mate," I said.

"Would it kill them to just..." His voice tailed off.

"Does it really matter, Steve?"

"Yeah. Probably." His shoulders dropped. "What am I doing wrong?"

"To be honest, you're being a bit of a twat."

"Oh. Well. Cheers."

"Hey. We all are. If that helps."

"Immensely. Thanks."

"Any time," I said.

It took a couple of hours to get the sofa dumped so we were a little late opening. A small queue had formed and there was quite a buzz, by our standards, at least, when Toni unlocked the front door.

"Welcome, ghouls," she said with a flourish as a small stream of the elderly and the dispossessed filed past her.

"The sofa's gone," a woman said. She stood by the pot plant and looked affronted. She had on a shapeless beige coat and carried a handbag that could have doubled as body armour.

"It's a crime scene," Toni said. "Don't get too close, Ivy. You'll get your DNA all over it. You'll be a suspect."

"Suspect?" Ivy bristled. Then she saw Toni's face. "Very funny, I'm sure."

Toni nudged my arm and said, "I'm nipping out for a fag. You coming?"

"I don't smoke."

She gave an exaggerated sigh. "For a gossip. Come on, you old queen, don't be dense."

"Enough of the old," I said.

She pulled hard on her cigarette and blew a fierce, thin stream of smoke into the clear, blameless air. She was attractive, I supposed, if one was into that sort of thing. Lean, neat, well preserved for forty-odd. Her face was a hard kind of pretty and, oddly, it became harder when she smiled. Her eyes were pure and blue and distant.

"He was your mate, then. So Brenda says."

"Hardly."

"You knew his age, his birthday. That's more than Brenda knew and she was the only one of us he took any notice of, or so we thought."

"Does it matter?"

"Probably not. But shit, I'm bored. You're hiding something. So spill it or I'll tell Steve I saw you and Jeremy in a cubicle in the ladies."

"I don't even like Jeremy."

"I know that, you know that."

"I'm pretty sure that Jeremy knows it too."

"But Steve? He probably thinks all the gays are in one big club."

"All the gays? Really?"

"You know what I mean."

"What a bitch."

"Well. Yeah. And?" She flicked her half-smoked cigarette into the road. "Come on. Tell your Auntie Toni all about it."

I don't know why I spoke to him, why I said what I did. In the months that Arthur had been visiting the library I'd never felt the slightest inclination to do so before. But on this particular April afternoon, as the working day wound down and Arthur sat in his usual seat scanning the racing pages of the local paper, I said, "How's it going? Arthur, isn't it?"

"What?" He looked up at me with, perhaps understandable, suspicion.

"You're Arthur."

His eyes narrowed until his face was all wrinkles. "I know I am."

His scent, vibrantly appalling, approached me. I tried not to breathe in. "Yeah, I…"

"Where's the big girl?"

"Brenda?"

"Where's Brenda? I like her."

"Gone home. It's just me. I've got to lock up and everything. Hope I can handle the responsibility."

"What?"

"Thing is, I'm closing up in a minute and you need to leave."

"Why didn't you say so?" He closed the newspaper neatly and placed it on the table.

"Good question." He stood with some difficulty. Then I said, God knows why, "I only live round the corner. Do you fancy a cup of tea?"

He was pulling his trousers up high onto his waist. He paused mid-hitch. "Are you one of those gays?"

"As it happens, I am."

"Oh."

"You're safe, Arthur. I promise I'll keep my hands to myself."

"You'd better. I used to box, back in the day. I'd give you a fearful clout if you got any ideas."

"Duly noted."

Somewhat mollified he straightened himself and headed slowly towards the exit. "Tea, is it?"

"Or coffee."

"Anything stronger?"

"No."

"Any biscuits?"

"I daresay."

"Garibaldi's?"

"None of them. Hob Nob's, chocolate digestives, some custard creams, I think."

"They'll do, I suppose."

"Good," I said, stepping carefully around his scent.

There's an old armchair in my living room that I've been meaning to replace for ages but before I could direct Arthur towards it he had sunk himself and his stench cosily onto my small and, if I say so myself, rather stylish sofa.

"Oh well," I said. "A refurb it is."

"What?" Arthur said.

"Nothing."

"Where's that tea, boy? I can't stay long."

I busied myself in the kitchen. I found myself using a green, ivy-patterned teapot that had belonged to my mother. I remembered her taking it from the high cupboard in the terraced house in which I had been born and brought up on the day that I came out. She stood on her tiptoes, reaching above her head. Her hand shook. She took her time over the tea, delaying the trip back into the living room where my father sat, brick-red, fists balled, coiled, the *Daily Express* folded neatly on the table in front of him. The fury was on him then, entirely justified in his eyes. Mother carried the tray through, three tea cups jittering in their saucers, chocolate digestives fanned neatly on a matching side plate. She sat the tray on the table and waited for him to blow.

"About time," Arthur said as I returned to the living room. He reached for the teapot.

"I'll do it," I said, a little more sharply than I intended.

"No need to snap."

I said nothing as I poured the tea.

"Very posh," he said, lifting the cup from its saucer and sipping daintily.

"They were my mother's."

"Is that so?"

An odd silence settled. The light was fading so I stood and snapped on a couple of lamps.

I sat again. "You remind me of someone."

He ate a custard cream. He chewed slowly, looking at me. "I've my own place, you know," he said when he'd finished eating. "I'm not a charity case."

"Tea and biscuits? That's hardly charity. Where do you live, Arthur?"

"Doesn't matter. I like the library, though. It's warm and you have all the papers."

"We aim to please."

"I like Brenda." His expression took on a different cast. "She reminds *me* of someone."

"Good memories, Arthur?"

"No such thing." His smile became acidic, his lower lip damp and tremulous. "All the pretty girls. All the…"

His voice faded, stopped.

"You were one for the ladies, were you?"

His face, sour and narrow, tilted towards mine. "You'd not know about that, would you, boy?" He grabbed a biscuit and ate it quickly. Crumbs fell onto the sofa. I hadn't noticed his smell for a while. I wasn't sure whether that was a good thing or not. "I cut quite a dash. Lock up your daughters, they'd say. Arthur's about."

"Is that what they said?"

He nodded slowly, his eyes becoming distant. "That's what they said."

"Do you have any children, Arthur?"

"How would I know? You've got to keep moving,

boy. Moving and moving, years and years of it. Don't settle, never settle. You settle and they'll get you." He was animated now, dentures snapping, words tumbling out. "You sure you don't have anything stronger? I could do with a nip of something to help against the cold."

"It isn't cold."

"It's always cold."

"I don't drink. My father drank. I don't."

His top lip curled. "He's very proud, I'm sure."

"He's long dead." Is ten years long dead? Sometimes it is, sometimes it isn't.

"Is he now? The drink took him, did it?"

"Not exactly." I placed my cup and saucer carefully onto the tray. "My mother stabbed him in the heart with a carving knife."

"Jesus."

"He was asleep on the sofa. She called me and told me what she'd done. Then she walked up to Thorpe and stepped in front of the London train."

"What the actual fuck, Rob?" Toni fumbled for another cigarette, lit it.

"No one at the library knows. I've only been here seven years. After it happened I moved and changed my name."

"Christ. What did Arthur say?"

"That's rough." He drained his tea and poured himself some more." It's my birthday soon. Twenty ninth of May. I'll be seventy eight."

"Okay," I said. "Well done."

"Do you think she'll make me a cake? Brenda?"

"Does she know?"

He shook his head. "You could tell her."

"I could." But I never did. I stood. "I've got to get on."

Arthur stood also. He filled his jacket pockets with biscuits. "How lonely must you be, boy? To have an old codger like me round?"

"How lonely indeed," I said, ushering him out.

Toni took a long final drag on her cigarette. "Turns out he was a bit of prick."

"Yeah. Pretty much."

Steve leant out of the library door and tapped his watch theatrically.

She dropped the butt onto the pavement and ground it under her heel. "Will you go to the funeral?"

We headed back towards the door. "Why not?" I said.

Duck Egg Farm

The first mistake they make? They shoot him in the chest. He's wearing a vest. Of course he's wearing a vest.

We scream out of the car park, almost taking out a pensioner and a young couple. Their faces, astonished and affronted, becoming pink and tiny as we tear away.

Denny is driving and he's good. His face is grey. "They shot him, they shot him," he says in a thin voice, over and over like a mantra.

My brother lays across the back seat, his shirt ruined, his hands clasped together as though in prayer across the black Kevlar. His face is white, white as bone and his eyes are fixed on mine. He doesn't say anything. He doesn't have to.

I hear sirens in the distance.

Kevin is a couple of years older than me. In the late seventies we shared a council flat on the Heartsease Estate. Our dad long gone, mum cleared off with a merchant banker when I was seventeen. She was cleaning for him so it was pretty aspirational. Thatcher would have been proud.

Punk was big in Norwich then. It didn't do much for me but Kev loved it and dragged me along to gigs at *The Golden Star* and *Bedford's* and West Runton pavilion. I liked them. I enjoyed the booze and the fights and the girls and the sense that anything could happen, that everything was tearing apart at the seams. It was all bollocks, of course, but that didn't matter to a stupid seventeen-year-old like me.

But what Kev really loved was the counterculture. His words not mine, because I know just how wanky that sounds. I remember him saying exactly that, holding court in our tiny flat, the room stuffed with students and drop outs and thin, stoned girls, all piercings and long, lank hair. He was passing a joint round, the air drenched with pot, the stink of it, sweet and acrid and suffocating. Yeah, Kev loved the counterculture.

We drive north. Denny is quiet now because Kev told him to shut the fuck up and Denny is loyal and always does as he is told. It doesn't take long to reach the countryside from the city centre. It's a hot, dry August and the wheatfields are baked and pale and blurred as they shoot past the passenger window. It's wound down and I can feel the metal burning through the sleeve of my shirt.

"I don't know where I'm going," Denny says.

"Sure you do," I say.

"What does it matter?" Kev says. "We're all dead anyway."

I can see from Denny's face that he's trying to take it all in. He has open, expressive features, easily read. He's younger than us, the son of an old friend, many years gone. Everyone likes Denny. He looks angelic and he's quick to smile, eager to agree with anyone about anything. I've seen him kill, though, with his hands, with a knife. When he needed to. When he was told to. Every organisation needs a Denny.

Kev isn't looking at me any more. He isn't looking at anything. His complexion is the colour of curdled milk. He sneezes twice, suddenly, violently.

"Shut the window, Terry," he says. "Fucking hay fever."

I do as I'm told. We pass fields of rape, dazzling, iridescent yellow. We turn off the dual carriageway. The road is narrow and gets narrower. We hammer through a tiny village, crest the merest rise and then the horizon becomes utterly flat and empty.

We bought our drugs from a guy called Miller. He lived in a basement flat in a Victorian terraced house on Unthank Road that he shared with a tiny, timid wife and a child of indeterminate age and background. The area is gentrified now, becoming affluent. It wasn't then. But he was a professional man, an ex-teacher who gave private tuition in Maths and Physics from an office leant to him by a customer. He was affable and approachable. He wore a suit, with a waistcoat and no tie and, occasionally, carpet slippers on his feet. He had stunning body odour. It was like a punch, a physical thing, a presence that followed him everywhere and rarely left when he did. I wasn't aware that anyone ever mentioned it to him. Didn't want to hurt his feelings, I suppose, and it's never a great idea to offend your dealer.

It was a dull, chilly day towards the end of the decade when we met him for the last time. He was at *The Otter*, a rundown shithole of a pub around the corner from his house. It's long gone now, forgotten, unmourned, like so much from that time and this city.

Without preamble he handed us a shabby, mock-leather bound notebook.

"It's yours now, boys. I'm done."

"What?" I said. I just wanted some pot, a couple of pints.

Kev took the book and opened it. Names, phone numbers, some crossed out. Some notes in Millers's neat, clear, almost ornate handwriting.

"You're bright lads. I've been watching you." He was speaking mostly to Kev. I was just about clever enough to know how fucking stupid I was. "Either way, tomorrow I'm gone."

"What happened?" Kev said. He was trying to breathe through his mouth. We both were.

The bar was empty except for us but Miller paused before he spoke and checked behind him. "Coke deal," he whispered. "Me and some friends put a grand in each. Easy money they said. Time to branch out." He shook his head. "Some big lads from Essex got wind of it, just strolled up and took the lot."

"Anybody hurt?" Kev said.

"Not this time. No need." He looked ashamed and a little broken. "My advice? Just stick to the dope. Plenty of money in it. No need to get greedy."

"Where will you go?" I said.

Kev looked at me. "For fuck's sake, Terry."

Miller grinned. "I'm inclined to keep that to myself. No offense."

"We'll miss you," I said. I felt Kev's eyes on me again but he grunted his assent.

"I'm actually touched," Miller said, and he looked as though he meant it. He was a pretty good guy for a drug dealer. Even if he did stink.

He lasted two years. They found his body, along with that of his wife and kid, in a caravan on the outskirts of Rhyll. They'd been tied up and shot.

*

46

Duck Egg Farm lies between two tiny villages and within a small wooded area five miles from the North Norfolk coast. It's ours. Well, Kev's. Not that you will find his name anywhere on the paperwork. He bought it in the early nineties.

"For a rainy day," he said.

I didn't question it. By that time there was no point questioning Kev about anything.

It hasn't been a working farm since the fifties. It's just a cluster of barns and outbuildings and a small patchwork of old fields, turned to rubble and dust. We used one of the barns for storage briefly. We use the fields for other things.

We approach it now, along a dust track, ridged and hard as concrete. Kev sits up. The vest is off and his wrecked shirt barely covers the purpled, angry flesh.

"What's the plan?" I say.

He doesn't speak. Denny's head jerks between me and Kev and the road. He looks close to tears.

"This that rainy day, is it?" I say.

"What the fuck are you talking about?" Kev says.

Denny steers between two ancient gateposts and negotiates a short driveway, breaks sharply and stops next to an old pig pen. He cuts the engine and it is suddenly shockingly quiet. We crank the doors open and step into the baking air.

It was easy. Or perhaps Kev made it seem easy. That first evening, after we left Miller, the stink of him still on us, would be for days, he sat at the Formica-topped table in our kitchen and read the notebook cover to cover.

"Piece of piss," he said.

"If you say so."

He tilted the book towards me. "We know most of these guys. Or knew, in some cases."

"Can I quit my job?"

"What?"

"At the printers. I hate it. You know that." Indeed I did. Although it wasn't a bad job, not really. But I didn't want to get up at seven every morning and do the same thing over and over. I wanted permanently free weekends. Who doesn't?

Kev almost smiled as he looked at me. But he had shark's eyes. Utterly black, depthless. Even then, when he was young and relatively mellow. "And what use will you be, little brother? To warrant a wage, that is?"

I bristled, or tried to. "I'll be the muscle."

He laughed. A rare thing but surprisingly rich and deep and genuine. "You look the part, I suppose."

Which was true. If you didn't know me. I was tall and broad. I had muscles, although I had no idea where they came from and no clue how to use them. I looked like a right moody bastard as well, apparently. So I was told. "You always look so mean," a girlfriend once said, her fingers running down my cheek. She had that little smile she always had. As though she knew something you didn't. Which she probably did, on reflection. I don't remember her name.

So that was me. Granite on the outside. As soft as whipped cream underneath. Still am really. Despite all the evidence to the contrary.

And Kev? Well, he was the runt. Not that anyone ever said that. Not to his face. I had a good foot on him and he was slightly built, but whenever we walked into a room together it was Kev that drew the gaze. Reputation, perhaps, but even before that and after, with strangers. His features were almost pleasant at first glance, in an empty, meaningless way, but they quickly became smooth and blank and remorseless. He had charisma, I suppose. A dark charisma. I'd felt the pull of it for years and was worn down by it. Despite my youth and the bulk of me, the closer I got to my brother the smaller I felt.

"Where the bodies are buried," I say. "Literally. All those trips to the farm. You and me and Denny." And the others, before Denny. Young and lean and feral. And nameless it seems, as hard as I try to drag their faces from the pit of my mind. All the way back to Denny's father. His name I do remember. Carl. That angled, seen it all grin. The hands of a craftsman. A carpenter once, he said, eyes sliding back at the wonder and the waste of it all. Now what was left of him lies in a withered field, beyond the pig pen, beyond his son's shoulder.

"You in on this, Denny?" Kev says.

"Boss?" Denny says, eyes wide and unbelieving.

"Really?" I say.

We're in a wide, ragged circle. It could be a stand off, but it isn't. It isn't anything. Just three lost men.

"The state of you," I say. Kev holds the tattered pieces of his shirt together. "There's a t-shirt in my gym bag," I say to Denny. "In the boot. Fetch it for him, will you? So he can make himself decent."

Denny does as he's told, of course. More surprisingly, so does Kev. The top is too big and he looks pathetic, but still. The bruises are covered and there's a little more colour in his cheeks.

When he speaks to me his voice is low and even and without inflection. "You've done for us all, you soft cunt. You fucking mummy's boy."

"You're not wrong," I say. I find that I'm laughing although actually I want to cry.

Just dope, Miller said. And don't be greedy. Kev took him at his word. He built up a network of dregs and strays and scum and he paid them well. He turned a blind eye to the skimming and the stealing. Natural wastage, he called it. The devil's share. There was still plenty left, more than enough. It was a small price to pay for a grubby human buffer, for layers of cover and deniability. The cast was ever-changing, a constant churn of low lives and wannabes, with only three constants for those first ten years. The good years, as it turned out.

Me, Hugo and Fin.

Hugo was an ex-lawyer, educated and with a veneer of respectability. A posh voice went a long way in Norwich in those days. He was disgraced, dissolute, but he had contacts and Kev liked him. As much as he liked anyone.

Fin was an Irishman, fresh from the Troubles. So he said. At least we think he did. His accent was so impenetrable and his manner so vague we never knew if he was a Provo or a Unionist. But he was hard. Genuinely so, not like me. And he seemed loyal, probably because he was so surprised that Kev took him on, trusted him. Kev never asked how Fin had washed up in a Norwich squat, never cared about what he had done, what caused the emptiness that settled behind his eyes after a drink or two.

He was the real muscle, although in those first years there was little need for violence. We were dealing soft drugs in Norwich, a soft city. It had its underbelly, of course, every city does. But it was shallow and mild compared to most. And we wore discount store clothes, drove second hand cars. We lived in flats and ex-council houses. Kev quietly shovelled our cash into property, in the city centre and the North Norfolk coast. Hugo helped. It was a low key and shabby portfolio. Our names weren't on the deeds. No one noticed, no one cared. He bought a handful of legitimate businesses as well. A tattoo parlour, a laundrette, a bakery in the middle of Wells. A veneer of respectability, a little light money laundering. Kev kept the lowest of profiles. And everyone in Norwich knew who he was. It was quite a trick, really.

"I'm going into the barn," Kev says. "I'm sweating like a rapist out here."

We follow. There are holes in the roof and sunlight slants in, scattering the shadows. It's much cooler inside. It's mostly empty but there are some old wooden chairs and a pine table and we sit at it, across from each other.

"You going to answer that?" Kev says.

The phone in my pocket is set to silent but it's been pulsing against my thigh at regular intervals since we left the car park.

"Not yet," I say. "Where's yours?"

"Lost it when I was shot." He fixes me with his shark's eyes. "Should have gone for my head. Amateurs."

"Terry?" Denny says. I find his gaze much harder to take than my brother's. Those hurt, puppy eyes. But he has a gun pointed at my face so that takes the edge off a bit.

Ironically I still had the early mornings. Not always, not often but the hours were far from civilised. Shivering at Wells dockside before dawn, Fin silent as ever beside me, smoking constantly. Pick ups at dusk at tiny airfields in the depths of Norfolk. Meetings at warehouses and in dead empty spaces. I did most of the driving in those days. In truth, it was as dull as the printers. The waiting, the silences.

But I had days to myself as well, long languid days, with nothing to do and nobody to worry about except myself. I cut out the weed. Not a conscious decision, it just happened. So did Kev, coincidently, at about the same time. I started reading. Just any old crap at first. Dirt cheap paperbacks from post offices and charity shops. I stumbled across science fiction and consumed all the Asimov I could find, then Bradbury, Huxley, Vonnegut and then a zig-zag through Orwell, Nabokov, Bernard Malamud. Then Chandler, Hammett and Ross Macdonald. This was my new drug and I was utterly hooked.

Kev sneered. Of course he did. He read the *Express*, the *Sun* and, occasionally, the *Financial Times*. Hugo would borrow a paperback occasionally. He had a particular weakness for Stephen King, I remember. Fin simply couldn't give a shit.

But they were the best times, for me. On the beach at Wells, or in one of our Norwich flats, winter outside, dark and cold, but inside I would be lost in another world, somewhere much more vivid and real than this one.

"What did you do, Terry?" Denny says.

"It's a reasonable question," Kev says.

"Could you point the gun somewhere else?" I say. Apparently he can't. I remember that I'm halfway through Dennis Lehane's latest. I wonder how it ends.

*

For quite a long while Kev was not a monster. He wasn't good either, not remotely, but he wasn't cruel, at least not unnecessarily so and he didn't hurt anyone who didn't deserve it.

Then mum came back.

That summer I was living mostly in a rundown ex-council house on Dereham Road. It was a quiet afternoon and the living room was shaded and cool. I was laying across the sofa, deep into *Schindler's Ark* when the door opened and there she stood.

"Terry. My lovely boy. Are you going to give your old mum a hug?"

"Fucking hell," I said, but I stood, almost automatically, and took her in my arms. She felt tiny and frail. She smelt amazing.

"I've heard so much about you. I'm so proud." As though I'd been picked for the school football team or something. She pulled back, held me at arms' length. "Let me look at you. You always were the big boy, weren't you?"

"Mum?" I said.

"Close your mouth, Tel. You look gormless." Her eyes cut away from mine. "I suppose it has been a while."

"Fifteen years."

"Really?" She seemed surprised. "It's been hard."

"How's...?" I searched for the name.

"Ralph?"

"The merchant banker."

Perhaps it was the way I said it, but she gave me a look. "Make us a cup of tea and I'll tell you all about it."

Turns out that Ralph wasn't quite the catch he first appeared, although they had a few years before the cracks started to show.

"He changed," she said. "They always do. Men."

"Okay."

"And I think his social standing suffered a little. I mean, leaving his wife and running off with the cleaner."

"No shit," I said.

That look again, but the hint of a smile and I knew I still loved her.

Turned out that Ralph had been defrauding his employer. He was currently serving five years in Pentonville.

"Who would have believed it," I said, "A crooked banker."

She shrugged. "We're all bent, aren't we? One way or another." We were at the kitchen table. She took my hand in hers. "Anyway, how are you? Do you have a girlfriend?"

"Jesus."

"What?"

"I'm thirty-three, mum."

"I know. I can count."

"Stop speaking to me as though I'm a child."

"Well that's nice. After all these..."

"Give it a rest," I said, squeezing her hand then letting it go. "Look, it's good to see you. Surprisingly so, actually. But cut the bullshit. This is about money, isn't it?"

She didn't deny it. Which was good. She sat back in her chair, made a face. "I am a bit short. Fucking Ralph. The house has gone. Mortgaged to the hilt, of course." Her gaze flicked around the scruffy kitchen. "It was nice." Her nose wrinkled. "Nicer than this."

"You don't have to stay."

"I didn't mean it like that," she said quickly. "It's just...I'd heard that you were doing so well."

"We are. We have loads of these."

"Just like this?"

"Some worse. Some better. A little, at least."

"Really? Then what's the point?" I didn't have an answer for that. "I suppose Kevin's set himself up in a mansion somewhere."

"Hardly. He's living in King's Lynn at the moment. Basement flat, nothing special." I glanced at my watch. "Shit." The mention of his name snapped me back into reality, "He's picking me up in a bit. You'd better make a move."

"Why? I want to see him. He's my..."

"Look. Kev. He's not as easy going as me."

"Well, he never was, but..."

It was too late. We heard the car pull up then his profile loomed through the back door's frosted glass. He pulled it open and stood in the doorway. He did an almost comical double take when he saw our mother. Then he turned on his heel and slammed the door behind him. We heard him drive off.

"That went well," mum said.

"Better than I expected."

He rang a little later. "Is the bitch still there?"

"She's going to be staying with me for a bit. Look, Kev..."

He'd already hung up. We didn't speak again for months.

"What was the dog's name?" I say. I'm trying to ignore the gun. The air in the barn is green and hushed.

"What dog?" Kev says.

"When dad was around. You know, scruffy little thing. Mongrel. Used to piss everywhere."

Kev's face goes blank. Not an unusual occurrence. Then, in a flat voice, "Scottie."

"That's it. Scottie. We loved him didn't we?"

"Look, why the..."

"We loved him, didn't we? And then he pissed in the kitchen one time too many and dad took him outside and killed him with a shovel. Do you remember that, Kev? Do you remember the sound he made? Do you remember mum comforting us, trying to make it all better?"

His eyes meet mine. I'm still not immune to the emptiness there, the lack. "I remember."

"It's not all mum's fault. I know she left. But dad left too."

"We were glad when he left. So was mum."

"Because he was a fucking psychopath. But still. With you, it was all on mum. Everything."

"You finished?" He tips his head towards Denny, whose gaze is fixed on the table. The gun has gone, which seems odd but I don't question it. "Do you think he needs to hear this?"

"The point..."

"I know what the point is," Kev says. "This is mum. You and mum."

"We had some help," I say.

It was good, having mum around. She stayed at Dereham Road for the best part of a year. It wasn't as though I was re-living some sort of mythical childhood. At least I don't think it was. Our paths didn't cross that much. We tended to be out at different times. There were men. A few. But they were transient and I paid them no particular attention. For the most part, neither did she. Perhaps it was like having an older sister around. I wouldn't really know.

She never mentioned my father and never apologised for or attempted to justify her leaving. I was glad. We all have our reasons. Even my dad, however warped they may have been, however pitiful.

I made her dinner once. Just bolognese, nothing special. A bottle of red. We sat in the scruffy kitchen as the light dimmed and the radio burbled in the background.

"This is nice," she said. I noted the gentle surprise in her voice.

"Dolmio," I said. "I can't take much credit."

"Not just that."

"I know. But...whatever you're thinking, don't say it."

"Say what?"

"You wish Kev was here."

A snort of laughter and mum's usual voice was back. Warm, but hectoring. Sardonic. "No, love. No. I think that ship has sailed, don't you?" I was quiet for a moment. "What?" mum said.

I imagined Kev sitting there. Imagined the expression on his face. We were meeting up again, there was work to be done. But the darkness in him was growing, the mood swings were wilder and harder to read. The Kev of a few years ago seemed cuddly and carefree in comparison.

"Yeah, it's sailed alright," I said.

A few days later Kev and I went for a drive to Duck Egg Farm. On the way I tried to talk about mum, but he blanked me completely.

He took me in the barn. There were several crates and some of them were open. They were full of weapons, automatic rifles, small arms, ammunition.

"What the fuck?" I said.

"We're branching out," he said.

He led me back to the car and opened the boot. Hugo was inside, on his back, legs drawn up. His chest was an open wound and there was blood in his hair.

Kev didn't seem to notice the shock on my face. "He was ripping us off. I mean, big time."

"Of course he was," I said. "They all do. We don't give a shit."

He looked at me. His face was animated and he seemed almost happy. "We've been too soft for too long." He stared at Hugo's body. "He had to go. It was him or me. Really. If you think about it."

I didn't speak. I wanted to be anywhere but there. I wanted to be back in my shitty little flat reading *Slaughterhouse-Five*.

He rubbed his hands together. "We'll bury him in that field. Then I've got a job for you." He rummaged in his pocket and brought out a small handgun. "Fin."

"What's he done?"

"It's what he might do. We need new blood. People we can trust."

"Why me?"

"You're closest to him."

"I can't..."

"Stop whining, little brother." His voice was mild. He could have been discussing what to have for dinner. "You do it or I'll kill mum and I'll kill you and bury you both in that field. There's loads of room." He looked up at me. "And if you mention mum again, I'll shoot you anyway."

I took the gun. He nodded and reached past Hugo's body and dragged two shovels out of the boot. "Anyway," he said, gazing at the blood, the wounds. "Turns out it's really easy."

Couple of days later, at an abandoned airfield to the east of Norwich, I found out that he was right.

*

"Who?"

"Ralph."

"Fucks sake."

"You knew he was back?"

Kev nods. His disgust is palpable.

"Actually, I liked him."

"Of course you did. You dopey cunt."

I did. He was urbane and charming. And funny. He was good to mum and treated me with respect, like an adult. He reminded me of Hugo in some ways. I think of Hugo then, stuffed in the back of Kev's car. Then Fin, the faint smile he gave when he saw the gun, and the "you wanker" that he spat in a perfect English accent the moment before I shot him.

One day, as the new millennium loomed, Kev said, "We need to centralise. We need a hub."

"A hub?"

"Yeah. We're too scattered. People think they can get away with anything. We'll use that big old place on Victoria Street. All the boys under one roof. I can keep an eye on them."

Great, I thought. "Are we selling the rest?"

"Who gives a shit? Let them rot."

I kept the keys to the house on Dereham Road, where mum found me. I'd hole up there sometimes, with a book, with my thoughts, to get away from Kev and his new, ever-changing cast of monobrow Neanderthals. There are few people that I have felt superior to in this life and they were all gathered together in that shitty, over-sized ex-council house. And there was Carl, of course. The only straggler from the old days. The only one I liked or trusted. He had his own life, a wife, a child, but he stuck with Kev out of some misplaced sense of honour, of loyalty.

A few weeks later, at Victoria Street, Kev was in the kitchen, doing a jigsaw. He was concentrating on the puzzle. A thousand pieces. The picture was baked beans, nothing else.

"What is the point of that?"

"It is quite hard." He looked up at me. "What?"

"Look, it's time to ease off, yeah? Keep a low profile. It's not as though we need..."

"I have a job for you." He slipped an edge piece into place, his face a picture of concentration.

"I'll just talk to myself then. What job?"

He looked up at me with flat eyes. "What do you think?"

"For fuck's sake, Kev. Why?"

"I don't trust him."

"You don't trust anybody."

"Good point."

"I won't do it."

His eyes are still on mine. "Terms and conditions, little brother." He called through to the other room. "Carl. You're off to the farm, mate. With Tel. I need something picking up."

Then Carl was in the doorway, glad to be doing something. Glad to be out of that room. "No problem, boss."

I followed him out of the room, the house. He was speaking to me, but I couldn't make out the words.

"Turns out he knows some people." I thought of something Miller said once. "Some tough lads from Essex."

"And you trusted him?"

"You're mental, Kev. Have been for years. Dad's genes, I reckon."

"Easy." He tries to stand but finds that he can't. "Easy. Remember who you're talking to." But there's no heat in his voice. None at all.

I look at his face and for some reason I think of the last moments of *The Long Good Friday*. Francis Monkman's terrific score. The close up on Hoskin's face as the Irish drive him away and the synth comes in. A young Pierce Brosnan holding the gun on him, gum snapping, eye contact, that sardonic grin. Then it's just Hoskin's and the music and you see it all in his face; the fear, the defiance, the resignation. I've watched it dozens of times. The music swells and the saxophone comes in and then it cuts and it all seems noble somehow, romantic. But actually, he was just a thug. He'd end up being shot in the head and dumped at the side of the road. What's romantic or noble about that?

"I love you, Kev," I say.

The shock on his face. It's almost funny. For some reason we both turn towards Denny but he's no longer there.

We were in Ralph's house, on Newmarket Road. Not his house exactly. A friend's. A friend of a friend. "I have some money," he said, laconically. "But I need more."

"Don't we all," mum said.

They were on one vast sofa, I was on another. Separated by a large, ornate coffee table.

I could smell Ralph's cologne from where I sat. Something warm and expensive. He had mum's hand in hers and was stroking the back of it with perfectly manicured fingers.

"It's for the best, babe," mum said. "Your brother, he'll get us all killed."

Ralph looked sad and tanned and handsome. Next to him, mum seemed tiny and vulnerable. She'd had some work done on her face, but it was tasteful. It suited her.

I don't know how I appeared to them. A fool, I suppose. A means to an end.

It's so quiet. I'm waiting for sirens, perhaps a helicopter or the sound of tyres screaming, doors slamming shut, voices. But there's nothing.

We look at each other. Anger, fear, resignation.

The barn door is open. The car was visible through the doorway when we first sat down. It isn't now. And the sun has gone, the light is fading. But it's early, isn't it? Too early for dusk and only an hour or so since…

…I tasted the fear in my mouth as we waited in the car park. I hadn't smoked for years but I wanted to then, wanted to badly.

"You all right, little brother?" Kev said. Denny was between us. Calm, his face empty.

It all happened quickly. Too quickly. A black range rover, naturally. Three big guys, all suits and shades, clichés really, ciphers, but clichés with shotguns, the sound of them impossibly loud amongst the concrete and steel. The world blurred and tilted and I thought, can we rewind, please? Just a little. Can I think about this?

And then Denny driving, brakes squealing and the hot, bright air…

*

...the first mistake they made? They didn't make a mistake.

"The thing is," Kev says, "I don't own a vest. I've never worn one. Neither have you. Or Denny."

"No," I say.

I pull the phone from my pocket. The screen is smashed. I can make a text out, though. From mum. From a moment ago. Or an hour, a lifetime.

"Sorry, sweetheart." Two kisses, which was nice.

I try to show the phone to Kev, but it's gone.

"I know," he says.

All the days, I think. Burned away. Discarded like litter.

I try not to look at the holes in his chest and he tries not to look at mine.

His hand reaches across the table and I take it.

I think perhaps that I can hear music swelling in the distance, a saxophone kicking in. But who am I trying to kid.

Box

About halfway through their seventh session Laura said to her therapist, "Honest answer. Do you genuinely dislike me?"

"You're my client," Ingrid said. "It's your money, your time. I..."

"It's my father's money," Laura said.

"It's all the same to me, dear. During our time together I am entirely committed to helping you feel...whatever it is you want to feel."

"You didn't answer my question."

"Yes I did."

"She doesn't sound entirely conventional," Mia said. It was Thursday so it was after work drinks. The cocktail bar was Mia's choice as were the lurid, sugary drinks that sat in front of them. Laura would have been more comfortable in the pub around the corner. They had some decent guest ales on at the moment. But she couldn't tell Mia that.

"Do you have any experience?" Laura asked. "Of therapy?"

Mia's hand fluttered to her throat. Her nails were crimson and perfectly manicured.

"Me? No way. Mother, on the other hand. Of course, that was Harley Street. A gazillion pounds an hour. Older man. Very dignified. Quite attractive, if one is into that sort of thing."

"You met him?"

"He came to dinner. He was a friend of Daddy's. The circles he moves in, you know. He did the trick. Well, Daddy was happy, at least."

"And your mum?"

Mia's lips pursed. "Mother's mother. You know." Laura didn't know. Didn't want to know. "She has her moments."

"Don't we all." Laura said.

Mia looked briefly confused but rallied quickly and started talking about her fiancé. His name was Sebastian. Of course it was, Laura thought, when she first found out. They had a holiday coming up. Skiing. Biarritz. Laura had heard all of this before. She smiled and nodded in the right places, as her thoughts scattered.

"You do not like this Mia?" Ingrid said, sitting back comfortably in her large leather armchair. She had a yellow legal pad in front of her. Her hands were still, a blue Parker pen lay on the arm of the chair.

"What was your first clue?" Laura said.

"And yet you spend time with her? Outside work? Why?"

"At last," Laura said. "A good question." She was in a much more formal chair, directly opposite Ingrid. They were in the therapist's living room. It was eclectically furnished. Laura didn't like the chair. It was hard. It forced her to sit upright. "She is moderately beautiful, I suppose."

"Does that matter?" Ingrid said.

"It does to Mia. Although, to be fair, *Lancome* and

Dior deserve some credit here. They do most of the heavy lifting."

"You wear make-up, do you not? You take care over your appearance?"

"But I do it ironically," Laura said. "So that's okay."

"Does Mia know how you really feel about her?"

"Seriously? What do you think, Sherlock? If I could tell people how I really feel, face to face, like, you know, an actual adult, then I wouldn't be here." Ingrid said nothing. Her expression didn't change. "I hang off her every vacuous word. She thinks I love her. I am, as we have long since established, a massive hypocrite."

"Your reaction is interesting," Ingrid said. "It was, of course, a rhetorical question."

"Great," Laura said. "My favourite kind."

Laura spent the weekend at her father's detached cottage in a village set deep in the Suffolk countryside. Roses bloomed in a trellis around the front door, pink and white and lemon. The roof was thatched. When he greeted her he was wearing jeans with a waistcoat and a dyed linen shirt. His hair was too long, his beard an afterthought, but they suited him somehow. As they hugged Martha took her bags. Martha was a stout, yet not unattractive woman, of indeterminate age and nationality. She rarely spoke. From Laura's point of view she just appeared one weekend. To the unspoken question, her father said, "Martha? Oh, you know. She drops in from time to time. Sorts me out." He didn't elaborate, for which Laura was inordinately grateful.

"Sweetheart, you've lost weight."

"You always say that," Laura said, disentangling herself. Her father had long arms so it took a while.

"Martha, tea, then food. We need to feed this girl up." Martha bustled past. "This new chap...Ben? He's not looking after you.".

"I'm thirty five. I don't need looking after."

"The Hammond's are coming round later. Drinks and nibbles. You remember the Hammond's? And their son, of course. Daniel. Nice lad."

"Jesus Christ," Laura said.

"I suppose he looks a little bit like Bill Nighy."

"Bill Nighy is a very attractive man," Ingrid said.

"Cheers," Laura said. "Good to know."

Ingrid scribbled something on her pad without looking at it. "Why did you tell me what your father looks like?"

"You asked me to talk about him."

"His looks? What do they matter?" Ingrid put the pen down. "You're either dissembling or...tell me, are you attracted to older men?"

Laura nearly bit. "Nice one. Trying to get under my skin. Shake something loose."

Ingrid smiled.

Over tea and biscuits her father said, "How's it going with the new therapist?"

"Ingrid."

"She's lasted a while. Longer than the others at least."

"She's a terrible therapist and I actively dislike her."

"Oh."

"No. That's good. She's the only adult I can actually speak my mind to. Apart from you, of course."

"I'm not sure that's a good thing."

"Fuck off, father."

"Precisely. You are very disrespectful. I can take it, but other people..."

"I am a paragon of virtue with other people."

"I worry about you. This Ben..."

"There is no Ben, Dad. I made him up to keep you quiet."

"You have issues, Laura. Intimacy issues."

"Do you know how creepy it is, a father speaking like that? So what if I do? It's my business what issues I have. Perhaps I like my issues."

"You can give up therapy if you wish. I am not coercing you. If you are happy paying your own rent, of course." In Central London, on an admin assistant's wage? Well, maybe, but Laura quite liked to be able to eat as well. He reached a hand towards hers. Long fingers, nails neat and short. "I just worry you'll end up like your mother, sweetheart."

"She died when I was young," Laura said.

"How young?"

"I don't remember exactly. Four, five?"

After a moment Ingrid said, "I am surprised you do not know how old you were when your mother died."

"Does it matter?"

Ingrid made a note on her yellow pad and said, "What happened?"

Laura shrugged. "They found her at the bottom of some cliffs. She'd been drinking."

"Suicide?"

"No note. An open verdict."

"How did your father take it?"

"He was thrilled."

"Thrilled?"

"That's sarcasm, Ingrid. How do you think he took it? He was devastated."

"Did he feel guilt?"

"Let's not go too far. Doesn't really do guilt, my father. Mind you, moving into a cottage next to a bloody great cliff with a young child and an unstable wife? Not the brightest."

"Unstable?"

"The cliffs?"

"Your mother."

"So I'm told."

"You have no recollection?"

"She smelled of lavender. I remember her taking me for a paddle in the rock pools at Sea Palling. It was hot. I had ice cream. She wore a thick coat, despite the heat and did not move from my side. I don't remember love, as such. But there was something. Of course, I was very young and I am not a reliable narrator."

"Have you become curious about her, as you have grown older? How about your mother's family? What do they have to say, about her life, her death?"

"I wouldn't know. They cut ties after she died. I couldn't even tell you where they live."

"Does that not strike you as odd?"

"Who knows? Dad said that they were a strange lot. And that mum was a drinker, depressive. She never really took to being a mother, he said."

"He blamed her death on you?"

"One could see it like that, couldn't one? But still, he looks like Bill Nighy, so that's all good, isn't it?"

*

As it turned out Daniel Hammond was not repulsive. Laura was already vaguely aware of him although they hadn't spoken for years. The Hammond's were one of a number of influential families that her father kept in a loose social orbit. Tobias Hammond was a retired judge. He looked the part; tall, stooped, stern, with white hair that was plotting an escape route from his ears and nostrils. His voice was surprisingly high-pitched, his handshake limp. His wife, Elsa, was unprepossessing in stature but her personality overwhelmed that of her husband. She made eye contact, was tactile to a degree that Laura found uncomfortable, she ate and drank with lip-smacking relish. She interrupted her husband often, her hand on his arm, her eyes mostly on Laura's father's. He didn't seem to mind.

Martha, having produced plates of cold meats and pickles and tiny, homemade pastries, joined them briefly, wordlessly, then retired to the kitchen again. The others took their drinks into the soft, blossom-scented evening. There was a gazebo at the end of the long garden and they sat beneath it, framed by azaleas and cherry-blossom. Elsa was becoming more overtly racist and right wing with every gin and tonic. Laura found this mildly diverting. She had simpered her way through the evening, very much her father's daughter, impeccably presented, vacuously charming.

It's almost over, she thought. I can make my excuses in the morning, get away early.

It was dark when she slid into the conservatory to fetch more drinks. Daniel joined her. "Nice evening," he said.

"Nice," Laura said. "Yes."

Daniel had, in his own masculine way, been as deferential, as merely decorative, as Laura. She could hardly blame him for that.

"It's been yonks, hasn't it?" he said, opening another bottle of Estrella. He took a draught. "Must have been Jonty's do, last time we met."

"Jonty?"

"You know Jonty. Everybody knows Jonty. Absolute legend."

Do they? Laura thought. She wasn't entirely sure whether Jonty was male or female.

"Must be a couple of World Cups ago now," Daniel said.

"I don't really like football."

He tipped his head apologetically. "Rugby World Cups, actually."

Rugby? Better. "Of course." Daniel was not tall but he was agreeably built. He was dressed casually, although in a particular way, as befitting a judge's son.

"Let me help you with those," he said, taking his mother's gin and tonic. "Back to the adults, I suppose."

"I suppose," Laura said.

Daniel hesitated. "Look, we could go for a drive, if you like. Tomorrow. Or next weekend."

"Indeed we could," Laura said.

"But what about Ben?" Mia said. They were in a wine bar close to the office. For once Mia was hanging onto Laura's conversation. She loved relationship talk, especially if there was a whiff of scandal.

Laura had forgotten about Ben. That can happen with people who don't actually exist. "He dumped me. Hooked up with a younger model. You know how it is."

"Oh Laura," Mia said. She placed a perfect, dainty hand onto Laura's. Laura's instinct was to pull away, to yelp with disgust. She fought it heroically. "I'm so sorry."

"Thanks, Mia."

"Men," Mia said.

"Indeed."

"I'm so lucky with Sebastian. He would never treat me that way." Give it a year or two, Laura thought. "Still. Daniel. A judge's son. Quite a catch."

"I've known him for years. I suppose I've never really seen him in...that way before."

"How romantic," Mia said.

Is it? Laura thought.

"Tell me more."

Laura did. Most of it was made up but it was partly the truth so that was something.

"A boyfriend who actually exists," Ingrid said. "Interesting."

"Are you mocking me?"

"Would you like me to?"

Laura almost laughed. "Anyway, he's not my boyfriend."

"What would you call him then?" Laura hesitated. "You go on dates, do you not?"

"Dates," Laura said. "I suppose so."

"You call them something else in this country?" Ingrid was enjoying this. She was leant forward, much more engaged than usual. No casual notetaking. The room was hushed and cool, the traffic muted through the double-glazed window.

"We spend time in each other's company. It's not unpleasant."

"How romantic."

"Do I strike you as a romantic, Ingrid?"

"My point is," Ingrid said, "there is a man in your life. An attractive man..."

"I'd say, not *un*attractive, to be precise."

Ingrid sighed. "Very well. You have a not *un*attractive man in your life. Presumably in quite close proximity. I wondered how this was affecting your intimacy issues."

"Jesus. You just want to hear the juicy bits, don't you?"

"Juicy bits?"

"Sex. You want to hear about the sex."

Ingrid looked genuinely affronted. "Laura, I assure you...I was a sexual therapist for many years. These matters are like...a bowl of cornflakes to me. Nothing, Utterly mundane. Anyway, I'm Swedish. It is meat and drink to us. Natural. Normal. We do not have the hang ups of you English."

"Bit defensive," Laura said.

Ingrid sat back, smoothed the top page of her pad with a sweep of her right hand. "You are free to speak of whatever you wish, of course. This seemed like a development, that is all, perhaps a breakthrough."

"I can't talk about the sex because there hasn't been any."

"But it's been, what, six, seven weeks?"

"Nine, actually."

"Nine? In Sweden we would have been..."

"Yes, yes. Bully for you. You're not helping, Ingrid."

"Sorry. What I meant to say was, how does this make you feel, Laura?"

"Feel? Bloody relieved, as it happens."

"Wonderful news," her father said. "You and Daniel. I knew it. Such a good match."

He'd come to London for the weekend and they

were in a bland but expensive restaurant a minutes' walk from his hotel.

"Lovely Daniel," Laura said.

Her father's fingers snaked across the white tablecloth and stroked the back of her hand. She had been enjoying her turbot but now her appetite fled.

"You know I'll help, of course. When it comes to...well, a house, the deposit, that kind of thing."

"Jesus, Dad, give it a rest. It's not been three months yet."

"Three months? Your mother and I..." He stopped speaking, his fork, loaded with venison, frozen inches from his lips.

"Broke your first rule, Dad. You mentioned Mum."

He laid the fork carefully on the plate. He had on a formal jacket, a flowered shirt, a red silk cravat. "No matter. It's the future that matters."

"I'll drink to that," Laura said.

Her father's smile was thin and wintry. "Three months is...long enough. In the scheme of things. If matters are to follow their natural order."

"Natural order?"

He glanced at her breasts, her stomach. "You're not getting any younger, Laura."

Laura stood. "Good talk, Dad. Good.. .fucking...talk."

She ran to the bathroom. She bit the back of her hand and stared wide eyed at her reflection in the mirror until a thin ribbon of blood dribbled between her teeth.

Daniel was pleasant, polite, undemanding and happy to give Laura as much personal space as she wished. He also seemed entirely disinterested in any form of physical intimacy. He was, in many ways, Laura's perfect boyfriend.

The closing moments of their first four or five dates had been excruciating for Laura. She braced herself, in the front seat of Daniel's Cabriolet soft top, waiting for the inevitable lunge, the fumbling, the wet open mouth. It never came. He kissed her cheek twice, the back of her hand once.

After a month she felt a perverse, contrary sense of resentment. She wondered what was wrong with her. He could, at least, give her the opportunity to reject him. But such feelings were swiftly superseded by relief.

After six weeks together they spent a long weekend in Edinburgh.

"Was it romantic?" Mia asked when she returned to work.

"Very," Laura said. "The hotel, the gardens, the food, the wine. Deeply romantic." And it had been. Ostensibly. The couples around them seemed to be particularly lovelorn.

"And?" Mia said. She was trying to look lascivious but she had recently been botoxed so the effect was lost a little.

"And what? A lady never tells. But, Mia, I will say that it was wonderful. The best night of my life."

And it had been. After a stunning meal and a bottle of the best claret she had ever tasted she and Daniel had slipped into comfortable pyjamas, then read for a while before sleeping, back to back, for eight hours straight. Wonderful.

One Sunday, after breakfast at Daniel's apartment, Laura folded her copy of the Observer, placed it carefully on her empty cereal bowl and said, "Daniel, are you gay?"

Daniel inspected his coffee cup, which was still empty. "Funny that. I was going to ask you the same."

"Touché," Laura said. "I understand. And no, I'm not." At least, I don't think I am, Laura thought. "And it doesn't matter. Either way. I was just...curious, I suppose."

"Me too. You've been very...patient."

"Patient," Laura said. "Interesting."

Daniel smiled. He had a good smile, Laura thought. Warm. "Wrong word?"

"No. I could say the same of you. The thing is, I have no particular desires. Physical desires. I suppose you need to know that. It's only fair."

"Thank you," Daniel said. There was a bruise forming, below his right eye, from yesterday's rugby match.

"And you?" Laura said.

"Me?" Daniel inspected the cup yet again, then put it down and rubbed his hands briskly together. "Yes. I do have...desires." Laura's heart sank. "I need to tell you, I think. You are free to leave once I've finished."

Laura braced herself.

"He likes what?" Ingrid said.

"I told you. Being restricted."

"I don't understand," Ingrid said. Her Parker pen rolled gently off the arm of her chair. "What pleasure is there in this?"

"Honestly," Laura said. "I thought you were the sex therapist. I thought it was like cornflakes to you."

Ingrid straightened, gathering herself. "I am aware of the practice, of course. I just don't understand what he enjoys about it."

"Neither do I. I'm not sure that's the point."

*

The first time, she tied Daniel to his bed by his wrists and ankles and left him for two hours. He insisted she went out so she drove around for a while and let her thoughts settle.

"Was he naked?" Ingrid said.

"He kept his pants on."

"I see. And when you returned, did you..." She made a pumping motion with her right hand.

"What? No. For God's sake, get your mind out of the gutter, woman. He had a shower and we ate dinner together. He was very calm and happy."

"I see."

"You plainly don't."

"Do you?"

"Well, no."

"What did you think? When he first mentioned this...thing."

"Honestly? I was shocked. And revolted. He said I could walk out and I almost did." She remembered Daniel, his head down, eyes averted, his face the colour of brick, as he repeated, gently, what he would like her to do. "But, it struck me, as he spoke, how little impact this would have on me. I didn't have to touch him. He didn't have to touch me. I just had to...leave him alone. He was so grateful, it made him so happy."

"Has it been just the once?"

"Three times. Yesterday I left him tied up while I went to work."

"Okay."

"The thing is, I'm quite touched. That he trusts me so much. And to mention it at all, the courage that took. I'm flattered, actually."

"Flattered?"

"Yeah, you know, the trust thing? It's a bit of a problem for me. Trusting people. Being trusted. I thought you might have picked up on that, what with you being a therapist and all."

Ingrid ignored the sarcasm. "You trust him?"

Laura paused a beat. "I think I do. Which is extraordinary, actually. But he's so guileless. Innocent, even. Despite his habits."

"This has been good?"

"Surprisingly, yes. Mind you, I'm not sure about the box."

"The box?"

"I thought it was for laundry," Laura said.

"Well, it can be," Daniel said. "But did you wonder about the air holes? And the padlock?"

"Now you come to mention it," Laura said.

"And it is extremely sturdy," Laura said. "For a laundry basket. Inches thick, the sides and lid."

"So, he wants you to lock him in this box. And leave him there?"

"That's the size of it."

"For how long?"

"A day, at first. Then overnight, perhaps."

"Is it safe?"

"He assures me that it is. We have a...protocol. He can barely move, of course. Which, apparently, is the point."

"How do you feel about this?"

Laura shrugged. "It's as weird as fuck. But it's no skin off my nose, is it? We're having a trial run on

Saturday. There's no rugby so I'm going to lock him in the box and go to the pub for a bit."

Ingrid nodded and tried to smile.

The trial run was fine. Daniel was glowing when she let him out of the box. A bit smelly, but glowing. And Laura had spent a lovely afternoon sampling a couple of very decent craft ales. Good times.

By now Laura was seeing Ingrid once every two or three weeks. She didn't really see the point any more but her father insisted. And, quietly, she quite enjoyed their odd conversations. It was a place to vent, if nothing else. She had long since had doubts about Ingrid's status as a therapist, despite the certificates, in Swedish, that hung on her walls. She wasn't sure this bothered her particularly, but she had mentioned it to Mia.

One Thursday evening, over a bottle of Chardonnay, Mia said, "This Ingrid? I asked Daddy, who asked his therapist friend, who did a bit of digging."

"Okay."

"I'm sorry," Mia said, sipping her wine. She didn't look sorry. "She isn't a therapist. Her name isn't Ingrid. And she isn't Swedish."

"But apart from that?"

"What?"

"Nothing."

"I'm sorry," Mia said again.

"No problem. And, thanks."

"You'll stop seeing her?"

"I'm not sure. I quite like her, actually. In a funny sort of way."

"But it's fraudulent, Laura. She should be reported. How did you even get her details, anyway?"

Laura thought for a moment. "My father gave them to me."

"I see." Mia hesitated.

"What?"

"I do so hate to be bearer of bad news." It was odd then, Laura thought, that Mia's eyes shone with a dark, waspish glee.

"Don't be silly. I appreciate it. Carry on, please."

"Dear Laura. So brave." Mia sipped her wine. Laura fought the urge to snap the glass at the stem and grind it into Mia's perfect, botoxed face. "It seems that once Daddy started digging he couldn't stop. Apparently, Ingrid worked for the Hammond's. A few years ago, under her real name, of course. She was their housekeeper. Funny, isn't it?"

"Hilarious."

"Not that they can afford such trappings any more, of course. The Hammond's. A judge being a problem gambler? Who would have thought? Although I'm sure you know all about that, what with your father owning their house. But Daniel is such a darling, isn't he? It's not all about the money, as Seb is always telling me."

At dinner that evening Laura was considering whether to mention what she had discovered about Daniel's family when he said, awkwardly, his eyes down, "Perhaps at some point, we should consider..."

He hesitated. "Yes?" Laura said. She was half-expecting a proposal.

"Well...normal..."

"Normal what?"

Eventually he forced it out. "Intimacies."

"Intimacies?" Laura said.

"Yes, you know..."

"I do know," Laura said. "Thanks. But why? I thought you liked...that thing you do."

His eyes came up, met hers then flicked away again. They were in separate chairs, in Laura's living room. "I do. Very much. And I am so grateful..."

"It's fine, "Laura said. The weekend after next was a Bank Holiday and Laura had agreed that Daniel could spend most of it in the box. He'd been like a puppy since, pathetically pleased.

"I'm sorry, I know how lucky I am."

"So why the change of heart?"

"It's not a change of heart. I just..." He took a breath. "If things are to follow their natural order, Laura, we must..."

"What?"

"And we're not getting any younger. Are we?"

That weekend Laura visited her father. Daniel was spending the weekend with his rugby friends. She wondered if they knew about his...proclivities. She assumed not. Rugby players weren't known for their sensitivity in such matters.

Her father had his hair pulled severely back and tied into a ponytail. He had good cheekbones, she supposed. For a man his age.

Martha was there, in the background. Her father barely spoke to her, but he would gesture from time to time if he wanted another drink or something cleared away.

The weather was fine, dry and warm, just as it always seemed to be when she visited her father. It was as though his cottage, or perhaps her father himself, existed in some kind of tiny, beneficial micro-climate.

"No imminent wedding bells, I assume? We wouldn't even mind if you tried living together."

"We?" Laura said.

"The Hammond's."

"You talk about us? Together? That's so sweet."

"That tone, Laura. I sometimes wonder how you have attracted anyone at all." He was drinking his whisky in small, frequent sips. The louche charm was less evident this evening, Laura noticed. The flesh on his face, his mood, seemed pared down and close to the bone.

"Me too," Laura said. "What I don't get is why you give such a shit."

Her father stiffened. "You're my daughter and I love you."

"Ah. The robot voice. My heart is melting."

Martha materialised from somewhere and hovered behind her father's chair. It was a moment or two before he noticed her. He half turned and said sharply, "What do you want?" Martha shrank back into the shadows. "I'm going outside for a cigarette," he said. "The air in here is stifling."

"Those things will kill you," Laura said.

"You wish," her father said, as he disappeared into the garden.

It was a moment before she realised that Martha had slid into the vacated chair opposite her. "He is a pig," she said. As ever, Laura couldn't quite place the accent. She found the older woman's proximity and the directness of her words profoundly shocking.

"I won't argue with that. So why do you stay?"

Martha leant forward and Laura was overwhelmed by the scent of lavender. "Same as you.

Same as Daniel." She held her hand out so that it was in front of Laura's face and rubbed her thumb and two forefingers together.

"Daniel?"

Martha's laugh was more of bark, short and brutal. "Yes. You think he cares for you? You think he loves you?"

"Daniel?" Her voice was a whisper. Something stung deep inside her.

"I hear them, on the phone. Your father and Daniel. You are a sow. To them. To him. You are meat. You are nothing but..."

"Jesus Christ, Martha. That's enough."

The older woman quietened and settled back in the chair. "I am helping you." She stood slowly and stepped back. The French doors opened and her father entered. Martha had gone. "I think I've been overly harsh," he said. "Long day." He stopped at the drinks cabinet and picked up the decanter. "Another drink?"

"Why not?" Laura said. Her voice was surprisingly even.

"You seem distracted," Ingrid said.

"Do I?"

"We can sit in silence for an hour if you wish."

"You still get paid, right?"

"Well. Yes."

"By my father?"

"By your father. A very generous man, to invest his time and money in his daughter's welfare."

"A veritable prince."

Traffic ticked by outside. Minutes passed. "How is Daniel?"

"Daniel?"

BOX

*

The Saturday morning of the bank holiday weekend Daniel stripped to his pants and folded himself into the laundry box. Before the lid went down he said, "We've both been busy, but we still need to talk. About..."

"I know. Enjoy this first, Ben."

"Ben?"

"Sorry, slip of the tongue," Laura said and locked him in the box.

"Yes. You remember Daniel?"

"Of course," Laura said. Do I? She thought. Didn't I make him up?

"He was asking about...intimacy, as I recall. You were thinking about it." Laura said nothing. "But," Ingrid squirmed a little. "He wanted some time in his little box. So strange. I've done some reading, you know. Apparently, it's all about...Laura? Are you listening?"

"Sorry, Pauline, my mind was drifting."

"Pauline?"

"Give it up," Laura said gently.

"Shit," Pauline said, her posture changing, shoulders falling back. "I've had a decent run, I suppose. Better than I expected."

"You were pretty good," Laura lied.

Pauline fumbled for her bag, extracted a pack of cigarettes and lit one. She blew smoke in a fierce, defiant stream towards the ceiling. "Actually, I like you, Laura."

"I'm touched. You worked for the Hammond's."

"Briefly. They're good people. Not their fault they had to let me go. I assume you know about...their problems?"

Laura nodded. "And my father?"

"A generous man. And, how would you say it, Laura? Not *un*attractive. He might have control issues, though."

"You think?"

Pauline took another hard pull on her cigarette and tapped ash absently onto the carpet. "Why couldn't you just breed? That's all he wanted."

"So I gather."

"It's not too much, to ask, is it? I've got three. It's not that hard."

"I've always been contrary. Like my mother, I suppose."

"That's what you like to think, Laura. But we're all trapped in our boxes, aren't we? Really? Daniel. Me, you. Even your father."

"That's deep. A bit of Ingrid has clearly rubbed off on you."

Pauline laughed. She found an ashtray in a cupboard drawer and stubbed out her cigarette.

Laura stood and walked to the window. It needed cleaning. Through the dirty pane the street beyond seemed grainy and nondescript. The sun had gone. It would be autumn soon, Laura thought, pressing her hands against the glass.

Walk On By

The day after Maggie died I wrecked her flat. It didn't bring her back. It didn't help much, but I had no idea what else to do.

Her funeral fell on Halloween. Walking to the church I passed kids dressed as witches, ghosts, monsters. The graveyard was like a film set. A thin mist dribbled between the headstones and the day was still, becoming golden. Maggie would have loved it.

Standing by the grave the vicar looked distracted and too young. Five other men gathered around the stark hole. And me. We were all the same age, give or take and we all had the same expression as gaze met gaze and cut away again.

It said, "Who the fuck are you?"

*

One time, at my house, back in the city, Maggie said, "I like that you don't ask questions. But I hate it too."

I said nothing. She looked at the open wine bottle on the coffee table but didn't touch it.

*

There was a pub next to the church. Isn't there always? We exchanged names, the six of us, as we stood outside, waiting for it to open, our breath, our words, turning to smoke in the chill air. No handshakes.

It was a Norfolk pub, rustic and unreconstructed. If the landlord was surprised at the influx of customers as he opened up he hid it well. Inside it smelled of last nights beer. We pulled a large rectangular table out from a corner, dragged some chairs over. We bought our own drinks and, settling across from each other, waited for someone to speak.

*

Maggie liked opera. It came as a surprise but I was used to surprises from Maggie by then. We saw La Boheme at Covent Garden. I enjoyed it more than I imagined, which wasn't saying much. Maggie was rapt throughout. Utterly absorbed. I took much more pleasure from the concentration on her face, the wonder, than from the performance itself. At the interval, as we sipped tonic water, she hugged me suddenly.

"Thank you so much." Her eyes were clear, her smile real and vast. It was odd how the years fled from her face. Nothing there but the moment. No needs, no wants.

Three weeks later I gave her a CD of the performance we'd watched. She was at her sink, arms braced against it, shoulders down, hair dipping towards the washing up bowl. She looked at the CD briefly and put it to one side. She never listened to it, as far as I am aware. Not with me, at least.

*

David spoke first. He was the largest of us, the most imposing. He was tall, with broad shoulders encased in a good, charcoal-coloured coat that fitted perfectly. He had grey hair cut expensively short and generous jowls that were shaved more closely than I have ever achieved in my life.

"Gentlemen. A toast, I think." His voice suited him. Deep and confident. He was used to this. Talking to a group. Taking the lead.

"A toast?" Five heads turned towards the speaker. I sensed us all trying to fix the name in place. Steve, I think.

"To Maggie. The woman we've just buried." Pleasantly patronising, which I imagined being David's default setting.

"Yeah, cheers, Dave, I get that." David bristled. "I just didn't expect the company. Do you know what I mean?"

"And we're just the ones who bothered to come," I said. Steve's gaze snapped onto me. Pallid complexion. Bad teeth. Wiry, edging towards feral. He wore a polo shirt and jeans with a thin zip up jacket. I tried to imagine him with Maggie but couldn't.

"What do you mean by that?"

"And we're current. Presumably." Nobody contradicted me. "How about the rest? The ones in the past. At our age, there's going to be a past. Do the math, as they say."

"What the fuck..."

"Easy," David said, hands out. He was on auto pilot, enjoying this, ready to smooth things out, to take control.

"It is what it is," I said, looking at Steve.

"That's deep, man. Thanks."

Across from me was a West Indian guy. Zack. I liked Zack. Simple name to remember. He was balding with liver spots on the back of his hands. He had an easy smile that he aimed in my direction. "You're naughty," he said, "But," Steve was to his left and he turned towards him, "he's right. What the man is saying is, it's not your business. I'm none of your business and you are none of mine."

"Then what the fuck are we doing here?"

"We're paying our respects," Zack said. His voice was lighter than David's but it carried more authority. David, seemingly aware of this, tried to draw the attention back to himself.

"Thank you, Zack. Exactly." He stood, emphasising his height, his build. "So, a toast."

The rest of us stood, some more reluctantly than others, holding our various drinks in a ragged circle.

"To Maggie," David said.

"To Maggie."

*

We were in the park. It was hot and the light was brash and unimpeded. Everything was washed out, us included. Maggie refused to hold my hand. I was too sticky, she said, too sweaty. She was wary, alert to others as they passed, on edge. It was as though she was checking for hazards, for danger. Making sure she knew where the exits were. She'd been clean for a few days so I put it down to that. We were on a long sweep of grass that led down to a river. The bank was crowded and noisy. She steered me away from the water towards a café. We sat in the shade drinking mineral water.

Maggie said, "I can't do this any more."

"This again?"

She pouted. It suited her.

"Have you done something to your hair?" I said.

"At last. He notices." The pout fled though.

"It looks good. Suits you." It was shorter. Layered? Possibly. I don't understand the technicalities.

"New me." Her hand was steady as she placed her glass back on the table.

"I approve."

"How gratifying." As her head moved her eyes seemed to change colour. "I can't make next week."

"Okay."

"I'm taking some time. Working on myself. As they say." The words were rushed and they tumbled together.

"They do?"

"Some."

"I appreciate the heads up, but it's none of my business."

"Of course it isn't."

Above us the ceiling fan turned laconically through exhausted air.

It was winter before she called again. When we met, I held her, felt her thrum against me. She wore a thin dress despite the cold. Her kisses tasted metallic. In the morning we drank coffee in bed.

She said, "It's just you now."

"In this moment at least."

"Bastard."

Her gaze wouldn't hold. Her eyes were wild and I sensed her thoughts skittering, pushing at her borders. Checking for an exit.

*

We all sat except Steve.

"Cheers for that, guys. It's been a blast. We must do it again." He scraped his chair noisily under the table. "I'm off to get myself tested. I suggest you all do the same." He tried to make an exit but the door stuck and he had to pull at it three times before it opened. "Fucker," he said as he tumbled out. The door hung open until the landlord plodded over patiently and closed it.

Next to me, to my right, Ray said, "Nice guy. I like him."

Zack snorted, then we all did. The brief, nervous laughter, and Steve's absence, seemed to dissipate the tension.

Across from Ray, Phil said, "Maybe he has a point, though? About the testing? No offence. To Maggie, or to you guys." Phil was slender with a quiet, cultured voice. He had thin features, hollow cheeks, a prominent Adam's apple that flexed frantically whether he was speaking or not.

"I'm all over that stuff," Zack said, giving Phil his full attention. "No illusions on that score. Know what I mean?" Phil's eyes were pale and watery behind circular spectacles. He looked at Zack without blinking. "Apparently not," Zack said.

Phil glanced at each of us in turn. "Just Steve and I, then. You must all think me very foolish."

"Not at all," David said. He seemed to mean it and I almost liked him. "We're all in the same boat here."

"What boat is that?" Ray said. "The Titanic?" After a moment. "And where are the lifeboats."

The door that the landlord had so carefully closed a moment ago burst open again. A youngish man entered along with a brief shot of chill air. His eyes found the five of us and fixed on me.

He pointed. "Right. Which one of you old cunts killed my mum?"

*

"He was a hard boy to love," Maggie said. It came from nowhere and I had no idea who she was talking about. A lover, I assumed. We were at hers, drinking wine, listening to a mix tape that an old boyfriend made for her years ago. Perry Como, Andy Williams, some Dean Martin. I hated it but it seemed to calm her. That and the wine.

Something by Sinatra came on. Fly me to the Moon.

"That's a bit better," I said.

"He was a bastard though. Wasn't he?"

"We all have our dark side."

"He should have stuck with Ava."

"Love of his life. So they say."

"Plenty of competition. Mind you, that voice, those eyes."

When the song finished I said, "What boy?"

"Huh?"

"You were saying something about someone being hard to love."

"Oh. Yeah. My son."

*

He was still looking at me, still pointing. "I know you."

I squeezed past Ray, made my way towards Maggie's son. The door was open and I guided him through it. The air outside was bright and cold. He shrugged my hand from his shoulder.

"You're late, Dean. You missed it."

"What?" He had a full face on a slim body. He was older than I first thought. Late thirties perhaps. He had small eyes and a goatee of sorts. He looked good though in a slick suit. Not black. Navy, with a dark blue shirt and matching tie. It was though he was trying to look like a gangster. And failing. I could see nothing of his mother there at all. "Overslept, didn't I? Alarm didn't go off."

"Happens to the best of us."

"Fuck you." He tried to push past me, back into the bar but I didn't move.

"I'm sorry about your mum, but you can't go saying stuff like that."

He took a step back, eyes flailing. He squinted against the low sun. "I just did."

"Really? How old are you?"

He was cowed slightly, the adrenaline ebbing. "It's not right, is all."

"No. It isn't."

"It's not fair." He did look young then, despite the facial hair, the sharp suit, the attitude. I almost wanted to hug him. Almost.

"I know. I'm sorry you missed it."

"Yeah. Well. All the stuff *she* missed." As though regretting the squirt of bitterness his expression tightened again. I sensed him gathering himself, tensing. Then Ray was there. Gingerly, perhaps. Belatedly. But there. He stood by my side, said to Dean, "All right? Sorry about your mum."

I swept a hand from one to the other. "Dean. Ray. Ray. Dean."

"I'm not shaking his hand," Dean said. Ray shrugged. "Anyway. I've got to get to work. You've not heard the last of this."

I pulled a page from my diary, scribbled a number, handed it to him. "Call me. We can have a drink. Or a coffee."

"Are you fucking kidding me?"

"Or not," I said. "Your choice."

He shook his head, cursing under his breath. He took the paper though, stuffing it into his pocket as he made his way to his car. It looked black and new and expensive.

As he drove away Phil came out, blinking rapidly, mild eyes watering. Then Zack, then David.

Ray said, "Here comes the cavalry."

*

"Even as a baby. And who doesn't love a baby, right?"

"Right," I said.

"I mean, he hardly slept. Colic. Rashes. Infections. Sickly little sod." She took the tiniest sip of Merlot then placed the glass back on the table. "The father was no help, of course."

"You can talk about him if you want."

"What's to talk about? He came and went. Nothing unusual about that. I barely remember his face, his name."

"Fair enough."

She turned slowly towards me. "Is that the sound of you judging me?"

"You know better than that."

She picked up her wine again then sat back on the sofa. She crossed her legs with a swish. Her skirt rode up and I looked at her thigh. "I suppose I do."

"Are you still in touch?"

"I just said..."

"With your son."

"Oh. Dean. His name is Dean. He's fifteen now, which would make him about eight when we got together. Should have told you, huh?"

"Maybe."

"Not my style. Not our style, really. You angry?"
I checked. It turned out that I wasn't.

The music stopped. She stood and ejected the
tape and tossed it onto the table. She considered more
music then decided against it. She sat heavily. The glass
in her left hand throughout, the wine unspilt. "They
took him away. I was an unfit mother, that was what
they said."

"How old was he then?"

"Four, five. The truth is I don't really remember.
Things were...chaotic." A quick glance, the shyest of
grins and hooded eyes. "What's new, huh?"

"I'm sorry."

"I mean, I *was* an unfit mother. The very
definition. Still am, I suppose. But I tried. I did. I know
it wasn't enough. Nothing I do ever is. But I did love
him. I do love him. In my own way."

"That's what you do, Maggie. You love in your
own way." Her eyes on mine again, sharp and wary.
"That's not an insult. It's what we all do."

Her expression softened and I held her.

*

We dispersed quickly, without fuss. Dean wasn't
mentioned. David looked vaguely apologetic as he
mumbled something about work and made his way
back to his car. Phil and Zack followed. Zack hesitated a
moment and seemed on the verge of saying something
but settled for a raised hand and a half smile. Phil was
wordless as he slipped away. Ray lingered.

"Well. That's that."

"Indeed."

Ray was pared-down, neat and compact. He had a
pleasant, if weathered, face. There were lines under his

eyes that crinkled when he smiled. We were still outside the pub. The door was half open.

"Fancy another," Ray said.

I considered for a moment. "Why not?"

He ordered a Jameson's for himself, a pint of bitter for me. I didn't need the drink. Food would have been a better option. But it was that kind of day, that kind of week.

We chose a different table and sat opposite each other.

"I miss her," he said, sipping his whisky, savouring it.

"Me too."

"You knew about the boy?" I nodded. "How about you? Do you have any kids?"

"No. You?"

"Three. Not that I see them. Not for years. Life. You know?"

I nodded again. I did.

He held his glass up to the light. "These days it's mostly this."

"You don't look like a drinker."

"Thanks. Good genes. Which I'm wasting, of course. Some days I'll start early, before lunch. Hit it hard then taper off in the evening. Other days it's long walks and mineral water. Not so many of those days any more." I waited. "The thing is, I like it. The way it makes me feel. Most of the time."

"More than your kids?"

If he took offence he didn't show it. "Seems that way."

"You're not alone."

"I very much am. And it's getting harder. At our age, everything is, right?"

"Pretty much."

"It'll get me. I know that. Sooner rather than later. My choice though. Whatever happens."

Two guys came in. They looked about twelve but were probably a dozen years older. They exchanged some desultory small talk with the landlord then took their drinks to the pool table and racked up with a clatter.

Ray gazed into his drink again. "The thing is, I missed her even when I was with her." He looked past my shoulder at the boys playing pool. Balls clacked together. A burst of laughter. A curse.

"I know what you mean."

"You do? I thought I was talking bollocks. As usual."

The beer was flat and tasted of nothing in particular. I drank half of it in a single draft. "With Maggie..." I hesitated. I imagined her there, sitting between us. The scent of her, her hand brushing mine.

"What?"

I sat forward, looked at him full on. "She had this way. She could seem intensely present one moment and almost entirely absent the next. In the middle of a sentence, between sips of wine. Did my head in, to be honest. But when she was there, fully there..."

"I know. It made up for it all, didn't it?"

"It did."

He shifted in his seat, let out a heavy breath. "If I add all those moments up, I don't suppose they amount to much. But...they were kind of everything. And I had kids. A marriage. It's pathetic."

"I don't think it is, Ray."

I got us some more drinks.

*

We were at a gig in Camden. It was a dive, spit and sawdust, a bear pit of a place. The band played a raucous blues rock hybrid. Maggie danced like a dervish. Sweat plastered her hair to her forehead. She knew the guitarist. He was good, as was the band. I loved the music, hated him. When Maggie introduced him during a break he shook my hand without looking at me. His attention was all on Maggie, touching her arm, her shoulder, her back. She didn't encourage him particularly. When they finished playing I saw him nip out of a side door, into an alley for a smoke. I followed him. It was January and freezing cold. He grunted when he saw me. I punched him three times hard in the stomach. He went down, puking, onto the icy pavement. When he could speak he called me a cunt, which I suppose was fair enough. I kicked him in the face. Then Maggie was there.

"For fuck's sake," she said, taking my hand. We were staying at her friends, a couple of streets away. We walked there in silence. She held me in the night. Her lips were soft and tasted of sweat and gin.

*

"So what did you think," Ray said, "this morning. When you saw the rest of us. Around the grave." He was five drinks in but his words were clear, his hand steady.

"I try not to think, Ray. I find that works for me these days."

"Come on."

"I didn't think anything. I meant what I said. None of my business."

"It's not that easy. Not really."

I shrugged. "Maybe. But it's been a lot of years. You have to learn something as you get older. Don't you?"

A brief bitter laugh. "I wouldn't bet on it." A glance up. "How many years? If you don't mind me asking?"

"Maggie and I? Thirty. Give or take."

"Fuck me."

"You?"

"Doesn't matter. Can't compete with that."

"It's not a competition. Anyway, we were very much on and off. Emphasis on the off. I was away a lot."

"Away?"

I nodded. He waited for me to continue but I didn't.

He thought for a moment, then said, "Thirty years. So Dean. He could be yours?"

"No. He was already around. But as I said, no kids."

Noticing the chill in my voice he raised a hand and gave a short, apologetic laugh. "Yeah. Sure. My bad, as the youngsters say."

"Do they really. Anyway. You and Maggie. I'm all ears."

"You sure you want to hear this?"

"Why not?"

*

One Spring a few years back we were on the beach at Brancaster. The horizon was all sky and sea. High above terns wheeled, sleek and indifferent. The air was salt-edged, becoming warmer. We'd hired a cottage close to the cliff edge. We had four days together, a rare commitment on both our parts. It was usually a weekend at most, perhaps an evening, occasionally merely an afternoon. For now we walked slowly across the vast beach, hand in hand, pretending to be a couple.

Maggie had grown her hair and dyed it blonde. She wore sunglasses and a patterned silk scarf tied under her chin. If she was aiming for an air of faded glamour she'd achieved it entirely.

"Our last evening," she said.

"Sounds like you're counting the hours."

I felt her grip tighten. "I am. But not in the way that you think."

"I'm sorry."

"It's been lovely. Please don't spoil it." It's what I do, I thought. "We should plan ahead a bit more. Try and do this more often."

"But we're busy people. How would we find the time?"

She let go of my hand. "Why are you being such a prick?"

It was a good question.

Later Maggie cooked. Nothing complicated. Shepherd's pie, cheesecake to follow. It was lovely. There was wine, of course. Whisky later. The mood softened. I softened. Our parting the next morning would be muted and hungover. I would feel how I always felt when Maggie left. Intense regret. Immense relief.

*

"We met through my work," Ray said. He cradled his glass in both hands, stared into it. "Five years ago this Christmas."

"Five years isn't nothing. What work do you do?"

"Did. Past tense. I was a copper." He looked up at me, checking for a reaction. When he didn't get one he turned back to the glass. "I made detective. Detective Constable. Briefly." He tilted the whisky in my direction. "I was drinking. There was an incident. Maybe a couple. But I'd put in some good years and they were kind. They let me retire. No fuss."

"But this was after you met Maggie?"

"Yeah. She was at the front desk, bollocking the duty sergeant. This was when she lived in Norwich. She was trying to report an assault. He wasn't taking her seriously."

"An assault?"

"Not on her. Her neighbour. Janet. Older woman, a bit simple."

"I know Janet."

"Yeah, good-hearted sort. But vulnerable. Probably shouldn't have been living on her own."

"Maggie tried to look out for her."

"That she did. Bearing in mind that sometimes she could barely look after herself."

"She was stronger than she looked."

He sat back heavily. "I know, I know." I saw the drink on him then. In the cast of his eyes, in his skin and in the set of his mouth. "Still, I took her outside, listened to her, said I'd help."

"Did you make a habit of that?"

"Not really. But you know Maggie. She was like a magnet. She needed me. Well, she needed someone. I liked that. The chance to be a knight in shining armour."

"You fancied her."

"Yeah. I fancied her. Not exactly alone in that, am I?"

"Hardly."

"But..." The edge that had grown in his voice subsided again. "I did want to help. Make a difference. God knows, I was making fuck all difference to anyone else by then."

"What happened to Janet?"

"Janet?" His focus was slipping. I watched him try hard to re-establish control. "A couple of kids were giving her a hard time. Well, I say kids." He tipped his head towards the pool players behind me. "Same age as those two, I suppose. They were taking the piss, nicking her shopping, stuff like that. Once, Janet tried to stand her ground. Wouldn't let go of her bag. One of them pushed her and she fell. Hit her head. They nicked her bags and ran off, heroes that they were."

"It was assault then?"

"Oh yeah. Maggie found her, took her home, cleaned her up. Janet didn't want a fuss. No hospital, no police."

"That sounds like Janet."

"But...no witnesses, Janet wouldn't report it. And with Maggie's record..."

"Can't have helped."

"Not really. So what could we do? Officially."

"But unofficially?"

"Unofficially? They were easy to find. They drank at the Larkman."

"Say no more."

A grunt. "A colleague and me waited for them one night. There was a lock in. It was a long wait. When they came out we dragged them into a passageway and beat the shit out of them. Told them why, told them what would happen if they went near Janet again. They didn't go near Janet again."

"And everyone lived happily ever after."

"Something like that."

*

It was a summer's day, but dull and threatening rain. We were in the cemetery in the city centre, stood by a grave whose stone held a name that I didn't recognise.

"Dad," Maggie said. "I come here every year, on his birthday."

"Okay," I said. "We could have stopped, bought some flowers."

"No flowers. I'm only here to make sure he's still dead."

"I see."

"No reason you should."

"You've never mentioned him before."

"Well, it's not as though we share everything, is it?"

"I suppose not."

She knelt and placed a bare hand on the scruffy turf. The grave was unkempt. The lettering on the stone was worn. In the row in front of us a youngish couple placed flowers carefully next to a pristine headstone and stood, hand in hand, heads angled together.

"I was forty before I even considered that my parents might have had lives of their own," I said. "Their own dreams and needs. They were both dead by then, of course."

Maggie stood, brushing her fingers against her linen jacket. Her hair was brunette, pulled back in a severe ponytail. "I never had any illusions about my father's needs and wants. It was all about him, always. He devoured us, my mother and me."

"I'm sorry."

"It's not what you think, though." Her eyes remained fixed on the headstone. Perhaps she was afraid that the dates would change, that the year of death would disappear.

"I'm not thinking anything."

"Of course you are. But it wasn't that. Not at all. He was just a bastard. An everyday bastard."

"Lots of them about."

"Ain't that the truth."

A shaft of weak and unconvincing sunlight forced its way through the low cloud, missing us by yards.

*

The drink had overwhelmed him. His barricades were engulfed, destroyed. The centre could not hold. It's funny how a face can change. I liked his features when we met; easy, open, quick to smile. Now his jowls were pinched and sallow, his eyes becoming pinpricks as he disappeared within himself. I thought of Maggie, into her third bottle, eyes wild, thoughts scattered, mothlike, battering against any source of light, of heat.

It was just us and the landlord. Through the window the light had almost gone. Maggie was still dead.

"It's all feelings now, isn't it," Ray said. "As if they matter." He put on a whiny voice. "He hurt my feelings. Poor fucking me." He looked thin and mean. I could imagine him off duty, in plain clothes, administering his own justice, in a backstreet, an alley. "Not like that in our day. Soft as shit they are now." A baleful eye met mine. "You haven't got much to say."

"It's the last bus to Norwich soon. I need to be on it. You going that way?"

"I've got my car."

"Seriously?"

"What? Are you my fucking mother?"

I breathed out slowly, waited a moment. "You do what you want. Just try not to kill anyone"

"You judging me?" I thought of Maggie again. "You're fucking judging me." A finger jabbed towards my chest. Spittle gathered on his lower lip. "Mystery man. Mister thirty fucking years."

I drained my drink as I stood. His eyes and his finger followed me with difficulty.

"Take care of yourself, Ray."

"Fuck off."

The landlord watched us with mild indifference, elbows braced against the bar.

The pub isn't far from the church. The bus stop isn't far from the pub. Nowhere is too far from anywhere in this particular market town.

The bus to Norwich was waiting and I took a seat halfway down on the driver's side. There were two other passengers. They kept their distance. No eye contact, no speaking, which was fine by me.

The driver ground into gear and gunned the engine. Ray boarded the bus with a grunt, then sat heavily next to me. His whisky breath bellowed over. He held a plastic bag scrunched in his lap.

"Last bus to Norwich. Sounds like a terrible film."

"I thought you liked the way it makes you feel," I said.

"Mostly," he said. "Today, not so much. Sorry."

"No problem."

It was fully dark. The heater in the bus struggled against the cold. Ray pulled a bottle of water from the bag and took a long swig. He offered it to me. I shook my head. He drained the bottle and tossed it onto the floor. He slept all the way to Norwich. I wasn't sorry. Condensation formed on the inside of the window. I ran a finger through it and stared into the darkness. It stared right back.

We came to a halt at the bus station in Surrey Street. The engine cut out with a shudder. Ray woke. He sat up, suddenly clear-eyed and sober. Must have been those good genes kicking in. He still stunk of whisky, though. The fumes washed over me as we stood.

"So what do you think? What Dean said? Did one of us kill Maggie?" It was though the last few hours hadn't happened.

We were on Surrey Street, opposite the Aviva building, the statue of William Bignold listening in. "Odds are against it."

"You think?"

"The coroner didn't seem concerned."

"The coroner didn't give a shit. Heart failure. No kidding. You could put that on any death certificate and it wouldn't be a lie."

"I suppose."

"I've seen it many times. With Maggie's past? Ex-hooker, the drugs, the drink? Who needs the paperwork? Who really cares?"

"The drugs were years ago."

"No-one gives a shit. No family to kick up a fuss."

"Apart from Dean."

"Dean? The Dean who was late for his own mother's funeral?"

I shrugged, conceding the point. "So what do you think?"

He stuffed his hands even deeper into his coat pockets. "I think there are questions that need asking."

"And you're the man to ask them?"

"I've got fuck all else to do. I've still got friends on the force." He waited a beat. "Well, *a* friend. I'll start with him. I've got to go back to Mendham anyway. Pick up my car."

"Good point."

"Do you want to come with me?"

"Why not."

*

The day became brighter and warmer after we left the cemetery, as did Maggie's mood. I drove to Ingham and we had lunch at The Swan. She drank pints of bitter tops with her roast lamb. She spoke about music, about films she'd seen since we last met, about how she would like to go dancing again soon. Sprinkled in between she spoke about her father in fractured, disparate sentences.

"He never drank. Not a drop. He was very proud of the fact. My mother did, though and who could blame her."

"He beat her. Of course he did. There was no pattern to it. He didn't have to be angry. That was the worst of it. He was dispassionate, detached. As though it was just a chore, something that had to be done."

"He never laid a hand on me. I mean literally. He never held me, hugged me, put an arm around my shoulders. Never kissed me. He never punched me in the face, either, so it's all swings and roundabouts, I suppose."

"I can hardly remember him without a cigarette in his hand. He stank of them. His clothes, his breath. Sometimes at home, when I'm on my own, I think I can see something settle into the old armchair opposite the sofa. I hear a match strike and smell cigarette smoke. I don't like being on my own. I've never smoked. It's about the only thing I haven't done."

"Mum had photos of him from the war. He was in the infantry. He looked very handsome in his uniform. He was a good looking man. Kind eyes. Everybody said so."

"And when he died, when he finally fucking died, mum wouldn't hear a word said against him. The dining room became a shrine. I couldn't go in there. So when she died I cleaned it all out. Burnt it all. Every picture, every last scrap of him."

I didn't finish my lunch. When we left the pub I tried to hold her but she wouldn't let me.

*

The first Wednesday in November we drove to Mendham, Ray and I. His car was a Datsun. It was old, beaten up.

The Norfolk fields were flat and damp, the light rich, autumnal. Ray was quiet. "Heavy night," he said. He flicked the radio on. Ed Sheeran, naturally. He turned it off again. Any words we exchanged were entirely anodyne. The drive took less than half an hour but felt much longer.

We parked near the green, opposite a duck pond. Ray hunched into his black donkey jacket. He needed a shave. We stood by the car, stalling.

"We should go to the flat."

"We could have a drink first," Ray said.

"Afterwards. I expect we'll need it then."

He nodded reluctantly.

Maggie's flat was in a courtyard off the main street. Second floor, purpose built. Pushing doubts aside I took the steps to the front door two at a time and pulled out my key. Ray joined me. Bracing myself against the state I'd left the place in and the conversation that would follow I opened the door and entered.

There was a hallway, a decent sized kitchen to the left, a large, open plan living room straight ahead. The bedroom and bathroom lay to the right of the hallway. All the doors were open. I entered the kitchen. There was a strong smell of cleaning fluid and disinfectant. Everything was pristine. I was glad that I had my back to Ray. I had a moment to compose myself.

There was a built-in oven and hob. A fold up table sat against one wall. Above the table was a large print in a dark frame. A Norfolk beach with a vast impressionistic sky. There was a black dog at the water's edge, half turned towards the viewer. I'd never seen it before. I'd smashed the picture that had been there. A still life; a bottle of red wine, some grapes.

"Is that new?" Ray said, nodding at the painting.

"When were you last here?"

"Must be two, three months. We went to mine, mostly."

"Yeah, it's new. She got fed up with the bottle of wine. A bit near the knuckle."

"I get that." He studied the print. "This is pretty creepy, though."

He had a point. "Old Shuck, she called it. Picked it up from a charity shop."

He shrugged and ran a finger across the work surface next to the sink. "Was this you? Maggie kept this place tidy but I was here often enough to know that it was never this clean."

I considered another lie but instead I shook my head. "Not me. The police, perhaps?"

"Hardly. It wasn't even a crime scene."

"A mystery then."

The overwhelming scent in the living room was furniture polish. A dining table sat at one end. A three seat sofa straddled the centre of the room, a leather armchair across from it, a coffee table between. There were some shelves crammed with paperbacks. A pine unit. The vases and ornaments that I had hurled, one after the other, against the far wall had not been replaced. An old fashioned television sat mute and dust free in the corner of the room.

Ray said, "There's no sense of her here. None at all. I expected..."

"To feel overwhelmed."

"Yes. Exactly. But it's as though she's been washed away, exorcised." I nodded. He could have been reading my thoughts. "I'm just empty. Hollow. Like this place."

"Which is worse."

"I think it is," he said.

We saved the bedroom until last. The double bed was stripped bare. A large pine wardrobe was squeezed into the corner of the room; a small wooden chest lay at the end of the bed.

The cotton print curtains were drawn. I pulled them across and opened the sash window. I'm not sure why. Although Maggie died in this room the air was neutral, scentless.

I watched Ray rifle through the wardrobe, the chest, the bedside cabinets. "Nothing," he said. "Weird." He walked back into the kitchen, threw open the fridge, the cupboard doors. "Empty." He closed them again slowly. "You sure this isn't you?"

"I'm sure."

He pulled a hand across his face, gathering himself. "I've got to get out of here."

"Me too. But I don't want a drink."

He joined me in the hallway. He put a hand on my arm and I let him. "Strangely enough, neither do I."

There was a cafe near the church, on a corner, next to a florist. It had check tablecloths, fresh scones on the counter, today's specials chalked neatly on a board on the far wall. It smelled of soup and coffee.

It was busy. We took a corner table. A bright, overworked girl in a pink sweater came over after a moment or two and we ordered coffee, no food. When the coffee came I said, "Did you talk to your friend?"

He poured milk into his coffee, three spoonfuls of brown sugar. He stirred it slowly. I fought my impatience. "Yeah. Tom. Good bloke. It's been a while. The time gets away, doesn't it? I kind of thought he'd be more pleased to hear from me."

"Okay."

He placed the spoon carefully onto the saucer. "No reason you should give a shit about any of that, of course." A radio played in the background. Other people's conversations mingled and hummed. He pulled a small notebook from his coat pocket and opened it. From my perspective the handwriting was an indecipherable scrawl. "She was dead on the bed. We knew that. It was phoned in by a Mrs Kemp. A friend from the church."

"Church?"

"I know. But apparently so. She was worried, Maggie was late for a meeting. Mrs Kemp said that was very out of character." We exchanged a glance. "She had a key. And no, I don't know why. Found her on the bed. Fully clothed. Looked like she was sleeping, she said. Peaceful. But dead. Still warm, apparently. But dead." He faltered a little, took a mouthful of coffee. "After that it was as I said. The police response was cursory. No signs of a break in. Nothing suspicious at all. Just some drunken old hooker, that's all. As I said. Who gives a shit?"

"Easy."

He took a long, slow breath. He squeezed his eyes shut and pinched the bridge of his nose with the thumb and forefinger of his right hand. "Sorry." He turned the page of his notebook and then looked up at me, holding it open. "You know this Kemp woman?"

"No. You?"

"Never heard of her." He looked down at the notebook again, smoothing the page. "There was no trace of alcohol in her system. No drugs. Not so much as an aspirin. By all accounts she just lay down and died."

"That make any sense to you?"

"Well...her liver was fucked. She had the heart of an eighty-year old."

"She had a good heart."

"I know. But it was tired. *She* was tired."

"So it could happen that way."

"It could. Perhaps it did."

"She hadn't had a drink for six months."

"With all due respect, you don't actually know that."

I sat back, my coffee untouched. "No, I don't suppose I do."

"Which isn't to say you're wrong. I can't remember the last time I saw her drink. Our meetings had become less frequent. One of the reasons, I suppose. Given my habits."

"She was trying to be...I don't know...better? I'm not sure that makes sense. She was always trying to be better, from the moment I met her."

"She changed, certainly, the last year or so. But this church thing?"

"I know. Mrs Kemp. You got her address?"

He patted the notebook. "Of course. Think we should pay her a visit?"

"I do. When?"

He drained his coffee. "No time like the present."

*

For about five years or so, in the eighties, Maggie sang in a band. They played blues, rock, a little soul. Mostly covers. The band was good, tight and professional, but Maggie was something else. It was as though she lived every word, every note. She had a great voice but when it strayed from perfection, when it broke slightly, cracked on a certain note or word, it was then that the skin on my neck and my back tightened and tingled. She was great, but she never believed it. A fan filmed one of the gigs and we all watched it back at his place. Maggie was rapt for ten minutes, we all were, then she said, "Who the hell is that silly bitch? Turn this shit off."

We thought she was joking but she wasn't.

There were a couple more gigs after that. Maybe three. But the spark had gone. Their last performance was at a festival outside Cromer. It rained all day. Although Maggie's light had dimmed she was still better than good. After she sang the last words of the last song she turned to the drummer and told him that she quit.

She informed me later as the rain gathered in her hair and freckled her nose and cheeks. I knew better than to argue. It was a shame, I said. A waste. She scoffed at that.

Later, at her place, I said, "It was watching that video, wasn't it?"

"What do you mean?"

"You couldn't handle seeing how good you were. It doesn't marry with how you see yourself. That's why you quit."

"Listen to Freud over here."

"Seriously."

"Seriously? Who gives a shit? The world won't mourn because I'm not singing any more."

"Some will. You *are* good. Whether you like it or not."

"Aren't you sweet." She came and sat by me. She was fresh from the bath, in a lemon towelling robe. She smelled soft and fresh and clean. She kissed me gently on the mouth.

"You can't get round me like that," I said.

"I think I can."

She did.

*

Mrs Kemp lived in a pristine, if dated, semi-detached about ten minutes walk from Maggie's flat. She kept the chain on as she opened the door. Sensible.

"Yes?" A small face. Lined. Short white hair. No make up. She was about seventy, I guessed. Eighty perhaps.

"We're sorry to trouble you," Ray said. "We'd like to talk to you about Maggie."

"Maggie?" Her eyes, sharp and intelligent behind a pair of surprisingly fashionable glasses, dropped briefly at her name. "I've spoken to the police."

"I know. We're not the police. Although I used to be." He was all charm, an easy smile that reached his eyes. "We're old friends of hers." She said nothing, didn't move. He turned the smile up a notch. "I suppose we're after, what the young people call, closure."

That got a response, at least, even if it was contempt. "Closure. Honestly." She stared past us, at nothing. "I know all about Maggie's *friends*."

"We won't keep you long..." I started to say, but the door closed. Before Ray could speak we heard the chain unlatch and the door opened fully.

"You'd better come in," she said.

The house was austerely furnished, all dark wood and densely patterned fabrics. Few ornaments, no television. Every surface appeared ruthlessly clean. The scent of polish and cleaning fluid prevailed.

We followed her into a large living room. She was straight backed, tall. She moved easily. The only jewellery she wore was a simple cross on a silver chain around her neck. She was dressed in a plain beige sweater and dark brown slacks.

"The convention is to offer tea, isn't it?" She turned in the centre of the room, facing us. "I don't want tea. Do you?" We shook our heads simultaneously. "Good. Sit."

Ray and I did as we were told. The sofa was shallow and hard. Mrs Kemp sat in an armchair opposite. There was a book bent open on the table next to the chair. Sudoku, I thought. A jigsaw puzzle was half completed on the dining table behind her. The room was cold.

She perched forward, hands together and rested on her knees. "Well?"

Ray pulled out his notebook. A mistake.

"No," Mrs Kemp said.

"I didn't mean..."

"I will not be interrogated."

"I assure you..."

"As you said, you are no longer a policeman." She sat forward a little. "You can dispense with the charm, Ray. It won't work on me."

"So Maggie..."

"She talked about you, yes. Of course she did. I know you, Ray. I know your type."

Somehow Ray still had the smile in place, although the wattage had dimmed. "With respect, Mrs Kemp, I don't think you know me at all."

"With respect, Ray, I think I do. You're a drunk and a bully. You had a wife. You have children. What do you amount to now? What is the point of you?"

"Jesus," Ray said. "Maggie told you this?"

She sat back, emitting a tiny sigh. "No. Well, just the facts. Maggie never said a word against any of you. Bless her. Such a sweet girl. But I've worked with drunks and the homeless and the feckless. Through the church."

"And what a comfort you must be," I said.

Her head swivelled towards me and her eyes locked on mine. I fought the feeling of being pinned in place, like a butterfly on a cork board. "I dare say I have done more good this week than you have in your entire life."

"It's a safe bet," I said. I remembered the conversation I had with Dean outside the pub. "You didn't make Maggie's funeral, though, did you? Bless her."

She bristled for a moment then settled again as she took my measure. "I know you too. All those years. Do you have any idea of the damage you did? There's a special place in hell for..."

"It was your church, wasn't it? It's the only one in the village, so, call me Sherlock. And it's what, ten minutes walk away? Not much of an effort for such a special friend."

"I was there. By the gate. I saw you all. All her men, gathered around. As though you really cared. Do you know how stupid you looked? She was gone. She was in God's arms. It made me sick to the stomach, the sight of you. I've been to her grave. I pray for her every day."

"You sound a little defensive, Mrs Kemp."

"I found her. Do you know what a shock that was?

I thought she was asleep. She looked so peaceful." Her hand went to the cross that lay on her chest. "She was cold. I couldn't wake her."

"You went back later, cleaned the place. From top to bottom."

I expected her to mention the state I'd left Maggie's flat in, but she didn't. "It was the least I could do."

"You stripped the bedroom completely. No sheets, nothing. Why?"

"They smelled of her. I couldn't stand it. I burnt them in the garden."

"And the pillows? The cushions?"

"Yes." She had drifted a little but she found the steel in her voice again. "You can go now."

We both stood. She was a difficult woman to disobey. "We didn't know about you, Mrs Kemp," Ray said. "How long were you friends?"

"About a year."

"Through the church?"

"Of course."

Ray glanced at me. "We didn't know she'd found God, either."

"Why should you," she said as she ushered us towards the door. "You weren't interested in Maggie's spiritual life, any of you." The contempt was back, full volume. "It was just the one thing with you men, wasn't it? Just the usual."

"Do you really believe that?" I said.

"It doesn't matter what I believe," she said. We were at the door and she was closing it as she said, "It's what Maggie thought, though."

Outside, after a moment, Ray said, "Fuck."

"I could do with that drink now. You?"

Ray nodded.

Her breath smelled of garlic and wine. It was an anniversary. I don't remember which one. Her smile was too wide, her eyes too bright. It was a special meal, or meant to be. It was a new restaurant. It had been getting good reviews, but it was chilly, almost empty. The service was slightly off, the food mediocre. I felt the evening canting, tilting away from us.

Maggie wore a red dress in a velvety material. Thin straps, bare shoulders. Her lipstick matched the wine in the glass that she gripped too tightly. She looked beautiful, timelessly so. I wanted to tell her that but the words wouldn't come.

"Most people do small talk," she said, her chin on steepled fingers. The colour of her nails matched the wine, her lips.

"It's hardly my strength," I said.

"You could tell me about your day. About work." I didn't bother answering that. "I have no idea why I love you." I didn't answer that either. "Still, back to mine later, yeah? So I can fuck your brains out?"

A waiter was approaching us but he turned on his heel and attended instead to the only other couple in the place.

"I've never made you do anything you don't want to do," I said.

"They should put that on your headstone. It's quite an epitaph."

"Could be worse," I said.

She drank some wine, picked at the over-cooked lamb cutlet on her plate. "Do you believe in God?"

I smiled at that and met her eyes. Her mouth twisted a little and some of the tension eased. "No. You?"

She played with the glass, her cutlery. "The jury's out on that one. Mum did. For all the good it did her."

"I cannot understand how an intelligent person can believe in...a fairy tale."

"Well, that's original."

I shrugged. "Point taken. But still."

"The key word is believe." She looked right at me, reached a hand across and traced a line on the back of my hand with a fingernail. "It's not about intellect."

"For some it is."

"Perhaps. Or perhaps they say it is. It's about comfort. Something other than us."

"Self delusion. A crutch."

"So what if it is?"

"Anyway, I thought you said the jury's out. You're hardly God's poster girl. Surely you either believe or you don't?"

She sat back. "Touché."

This time I reached out, touched her hand with mine. Our fingers linked. "I don't mean to mock. It doesn't matter what you believe or don't believe. None of my business."

"Well, thanks," she said. But she was smiling at least.

*

We were in the pub again. I ordered at the bar and asked the landlord if he'd like one. He appraised me for a moment then said, "I could manage a half. Cheers."

As he gave me my change I said, "Do you know a Mrs Kemp?"

That look again. Thin lips, hooded eyes. "We all know Mrs Kemp."

"But not as a customer, I assume."

"Hardly. It's rather she knows us. The village. Our business."

"She's a busybody?"

"That's a polite word for it."

"You have others?"

"We all do. Well, most. I suppose she would say she was doing God's work. If I was being fair about it."

"And if you weren't?"

"Then she's a bitter, withered old cunt who should mind her own business."

"Sounds personal."

"You could say that."

I waited. He loaded some glasses into the dishwasher with a clatter, wiped the bar then faced me, arms braced. "I'd still be married if it wasn't for her."

"Okay."

"Look, I'm no saint."

"Who is?"

"Right. But it was my business. Not hers. I'd have told the missus in my own time." Our eyes met briefly. "Well, maybe not. But still. We were fine."

"I'm sorry."

He shrugged. "Three years ago now. Water under the bridge."

Sounds like it, I thought. "What's her story? She ever marry?"

"Kemp? Yeah. Poor bastard struck lucky and died. Accident. Thirty, forty years ago now."

"She doesn't look like the remarrying type."

"No. Not Cynthia. Too many souls to save. Too many lost girls."

"Lost girls?"

"Yeah. Through the church. Ex-hookers, addicts. The lost and the broken. She has done some good, I suppose," he said grudgingly. "Creepy, though."

"Creepy?"

"She forms these attachments. Always women, any age. I mean, I thought she was just an old dyke, but I don't think that's it." He wiped an already dry glass very slowly then put it down and said, "I had the last one in here a few weeks ago. Distraught she was."

"The last one?"

"Yeah. You know her, mate. You and all the others who were in here after the funeral."

"Maggie?"

"Maggie. Nice girl."

"Girl? She'd like that."

"She was a good sort. I'm sorry about..."

"How well did you know her?"

"That tone? Really? We were having such a nice chat."

I was gripping my glass too hard. Ray called across, "Where's my drink?"

I started to say something, but the landlord said, "Don't get your knickers in a twist. We only spoke the once. I knew she was Cynth's latest project, though. Word gets around, place like this."

"She was distraught?"

"Poured her heart out. It was quiet in here." He looked around the almost empty bar. "Hard to believe, I know."

"It was Kemp."

He nodded. "Driving her nuts. Wouldn't leave her alone. She wanted her to pray all the time. Atone for her sins. You know, all that churchy shit."

"Was she drunk?"

"What?"

"Maggie. Was she drinking?" He hesitated. "It's all right. It's not the confessional. You're not breaking any vows."

"Funny guy. No. She wasn't drunk. She had two mineral waters and thanked me for listening. She left a tip too. A good one."

"Sounds like Maggie. Do remember what day this was?"

He thought for a bit. "It was a Wednesday. There was a Champions League game on. Chelsea." There was a list of televised fixtures pinned on the wall behind me and he peered at it. "Must have been the 14th."

Two days before Maggie died.

"Finally," Ray said when I passed him his pint.

A group of three couples came in, an assault of perfume and aftershave, braying voices, a woman's laughter. My new friend was busy. I recited our conversation to Ray, word for word.

"Are you sure you weren't on the force?"

"Hardly," I said.

"You got more out of good old Cynthia than I did as well. I was like a rabbit in headlights. Fucking useless."

"I think it's fair to say that Mrs Kemp is not an easy woman."

"I'm not sure she's a woman at all. She reminded me of an old teacher. I haven't thought of her for years. Bloody harridan, she was. Infant school. I thought I'd done a good job blocking her out. Until now."

"Flashbacks?"

"You weren't there, man. You didn't see what I saw."

We both laughed. Then Ray said, "It's a lot to unpick. But I'm not sure that it amounts to much."

"One other thing," I said. "Did you notice that Cynthia said that Maggie was cold when she found her? In her statement to the police she said she was still warm."

He sipped his drink as he processed that. "You don't miss much."

"Does it mean anything? She's an old woman, it would have been a shock, even to her."

"Less of a shock if she killed her."

"Can you see that? Really?"

"I dunno. Probably not. But something's wrong though."

"With Cynth? No argument."

"Not just that."

"But the autopsy, the report. No drink, no drugs, no signs of violence."

"If we take all that at face value, I agree. But I thought..."

"What did you think, Ray? What did I think for that matter. What exactly are we doing?" He took another drink and I watched his eyes flatten. "It's a distraction, I suppose. For both of us. And perhaps I thought I'd feel closer to her somehow. The more I knew."

"How's that working out for you?"

"I didn't know her at all. Not a great surprise, all things considered. But still. I think we should stop."

"It's a free country, mate. You do what you want."

"And you?"

He drained his pint and stood to go and get another. "I'll do what I want."

*

Maggie was sprawled across an armchair, reading "The Power of Now" by Eckhart Tolle. We were in a beach hut at Southwold. Enough room for two chairs, a small table, somewhere to make tea.

It was pleasant in the shade. The day was blisteringly hot, the light searing across the green sea, blinding and blanching and burning in turn.

Maggie had on shorts and a halter top. Her legs, stretched over the arm of the chair, were long and brown. She wore no make up. Her hair was pale and pulled back, sunglasses propped above her forehead as she read.

She was calm, I was calm. It was a good day. A good weekend, as I recall.

After a while Maggie threw the book across the hut. It skidded off the sky blue decking and landed spine down on the hot sand.

I looked up from the paperback I was reading. "Not a fan?"

"Load of bollocks."

"It's very big at the moment. In the moment. Appropriately."

"It's all very well. Being in the now."

"It's all we have. So they tell me. This very instant."

Her sunglasses dropped over her eyes. She lifted them again. "Are you taking the piss?"

I held my hand out, forefinger and thumb close together. "Perhaps the tiniest bit."

"Ha bloody ha." She stood suddenly, took a long draught of coke from a can on the table. "I mean, I get it. Technically. Living in the moment. Not dwelling on the future, the past. Makes perfect sense."

"I sense a but."

"A massive one."

"Not like yours, then?" I reached out and traced a finger across the thin fabric covering her right buttock.

She brushed my hand away. "The thing is most moments are shit. Most of my moments, at least."

"This one?" I said.

She held my fingers lightly. "This one's fine. Most aren't. I prefer a life lived in retrospect. The edited highlights. I don't want to savour the crap bits."

"But you do, sweetheart. We all do."

"Sometimes." Outside the hut a Labrador sniffed at the cover of the discarded book. "I suppose that's what red wine is for."

"Red wine and Leonard Cohen."

"Or Joy Division."

"Or Portishead."

"I love Portishead," she said, sitting heavily on my lap.

"Jesus," I said.

"Let's not bring him into it."

I put my hand on her bare thigh. It was cool. There was a bruise on her left forearm, its edges purple, turning green.

*

The year ran down. Christmas came and, mercifully, went. I met Ray on Christmas Eve in a soulless riverside bar. We spoke about nothing much for a couple of hours. Maggie's name came up, of course, but neither of us wanted to take the conversation anywhere. It was just gone five and dark with a cold wind rushing in off the river when I left him. He was deep into himself, cradling a double Jameson's, two more lined up.

My daughter called on Christmas Day, as she always did. The conversation could have been cut and paste from any of the last ten, fifteen years. The line was poor, static scarred, her voice distant. She could have been a continent away. She could have been in the pub on the corner that I gazed at from my kitchen window.

I was adrift in the grim hinterland between Christmas and the New Year when Dean called.

*

I met him in one of the pizza places on Prince of Wales Road. He was in a plastic bucket seat at a bolted down table. He looked up at me then down at his pizza again.

"I said no anchovies." He picked up something small and grey and held it towards me as I sat. "What does that look like to you?"

"Hard to say."

"It's an anchovy. Joint like this, you've got to get the basics right." The stony-faced man from behind the counter came and took the pizza, still in its cardboard tray. "Fucking basics, mate," Dean said to him, but he was already walking off. "Do you want anything?" Dean said to me.

"I'm fine, thanks."

The guy came back again and dropped what was possibly another pizza onto the table. "No anchovies," he said.

"Great. Thanks. Not so hard, was it?" He was talking to the man's back though and got no response. He took a bite from a slice and cheap, molten mozzarella hung in ragged strings from his mouth, clinging to his neatly trimmed goatee. He grabbed a serviette and wiped grease from his hands and chin. "That's fucking horrible."

"Why meet here? Why are you even eating that?"

"I used to run one of these. In King's Lynn. Cut above this place, mind."

"Be hard not to be."

He grunted his assent. "Got a soft spot for them. The shit in a tray merchants, as Mike Skinner once called them."

"The Streets," I said. "I think I've got the album somewhere."

"Colour me impressed," Dean said. He slowly

chewed some more pizza as he looked at me. "I get nostalgic for this crap. This was pretty much my diet when I was a kid."

"So what do you do now, Dean?"

"I sell cars. Second hand. Me and a mate have got a place out on the Watton Road." He sighed. "I know how it sounds. It's not dodgy, though. We're straight up. Well, perhaps we take a little cash off the books from time to time, but who doesn't?" He folded the cardboard container over the remainder of the pizza. He dropped it into a bin on his way to the counter and came back with two bottles of cherry coke. I could still see nothing of Maggie in his features, his manner, the way he walked. Why should I? She barely touched this man. Barely knew him. I felt a wave of sadness. For him. For her.

"I was surprised when you called."

"Me too," Dean said. He took a long draught of coke. It fizzed in the neck of bottle and surged over his nose and cheeks. "Fuck's sake," he said. He cleaned himself up and I watched and waited. "Thing is, I've been having a hard time of it lately. Not that I expect you to care."

"To be honest, I don't," I said. "But I don't *not* care."

Dean thought about that for a moment. Nodded. "I mean it's not as though her being dead really makes any difference. I never saw her, anyway. Hardly ever. She was never there when I was a kid. It was all care homes, foster parents."

"I'm sorry."

"Don't give me that," he said, and there was a flash of the angry man who had confronted us in the pub. "That's not why I'm here, not why I called."

"Fair enough. Did you ever know your Dad?"

"No. I don't even know his name. Could have been anyone. I think she was on the game around that time." He hesitated. "She ever say anything to you?"

"One conversation in thirty years. But no name, I'm not sure if she even remembered. We were years in before I even knew you existed."

"That sounds like Maggie." His voice had become quiet and awkward. "Did she mention me much? After that?"

I considered lying but didn't. "To be honest, no."

"Great. Figures."

"She knew she was a poor mother and she did say that she loved you, in her own way. That she always had and always would." His eyes when they met mine were guarded. There was trace of tomato sauce in the corner of his mouth. "I don't know if that helps or not."

"Neither do I," he said. "But thanks."

He'd eschewed the gangster look for a polo shirt and jeans and a soft, navy-blue jacket that looked inadequate for the cold wind gathering outside the plate glass shop front.

"Was that why you called? Try to fill in some gaps?"

"Yeah. Something like that. You're a link, I suppose. Of sorts."

"Not much of one, as it turns out."

He shrugged. "Not your fault. Not your job."

"You going to try the rest? See what they have to say?"

He laughed without humour. "Could take a while, mate. No offence but that little gathering at the pub? Very much the shortlist."

"I think I've figured that out, Dean. Over the years."

"I mean, I've got her mobile, her contacts book. It's

a big book. I'm talking War and Peace..."

"Yeah, I get it. I get it."

He sat back, planted his hands on the greasy formica. "Touched a nerve? If it's any consolation it was only you six left, from what I could see. That's why I told you all. It was just a text, I know, but..."

"It was appreciated, Dean. I appreciated it. Did you let anyone else know?"

"Nah. Had to draw a line, didn't I? There was all her girlfriends in there too but I think most of them were hookers or druggies. Don't want those sorts rocking up at Mendham Church do we? Got to keep it respectable."

"It's a while since I've been called that."

"Except Janet. I told Janet. I called her actually. She cried." With a guilty lurch I realised that I hadn't even considered whether Janet was aware of Maggie's death. His eyes became shrewd. "We met though, right? Just the once. You turned up unexpectedly."

"Schoolboy error."

"Could have been worse. Much worse. I was, what, ten? Eleven?"

"Something like that."

"The look on your face. I'd surprised her too. Ran away from the foster folks. Caught a train and a bus. I thought she'd be pleased to see me. Proud. It was Mother's Day weekend. I'd made her a card." He shifted in his seat. "You were alright, though. After you got over the surprise. Spoke to me like I was an actual person."

"Did I?"

"You don't remember?"

"Not really."

He seemed to wither, to shrink into himself. "Of course you fucking don't. Well, she made some calls, didn't she? They came and took me away. Got to leave the grown ups alone."

"Grown ups," I said.

"It's what I am now, isn't it? Pushing forty, can you believe that? I can't." He touched the side of his head. "In here I'm still ten, still looking up at the likes of you, trying to get someone to listen, to at least seem as though they give a shit." He drained his coke, threw the plastic bottle against the far wall. "Fuck's sake," he said.

As we were leaving he said, "It's New Years Eve. Got any plans?"

"Thought I'd hit some clubs. Throw some shapes."

"Sarky bastard. My place is on King Street. You can come round for a bit if you want."

"Sure," I said. "Why not."

We bought Jack Daniels and Becks from the 24-hour store across from the pizza place. The guy who served us looked gaunt and haunted but was surprisingly avuncular.

As we walked I said, "Your place is hardly handy for work."

"My mate lives nearby, he minds the shop. I do all the online stuff, drop in now and then. To be honest, it's not going so well. My heart's not in it. Not even before..." His voice tailed off.

"Well, the flat will come to you. I assume there's no will?"

"Of course not. I expect it's rented. I haven't even looked into that stuff yet."

"It's not rented, Dean. And there's no mortgage. It's in Maggie's name. If there's no will, perhaps even if there is, it will come to you."

He was walking quickly but he slowed a little and turned his head towards me. "How do you know all this?"

"I bought it for her. I paid cash."

*

Dean's place was in a converted shoe factory. Apart from the bathroom and a small amount of storage it was open plan. The furnishings were rudimentary and random. Three sofas of various sizes sat at odd angles around an upturned fruit crate that served as a table of sorts. There was an enormous flat screen TV, a miscellany of games consoles, their controllers and leads spread creeper-like on the bare wooden floor. In the far corner was an unmade bed.

"I like what you've done with the place," I said.

"Eclectic. Right on trend." I think he was joking. He grabbed a shot glass from the kitchen and threw it to me. He sat on one of the sofas. Five joints were lined up neatly on the make-shift table. He lit one and offered it to me.

"I'll stick to this, thanks," I said as I sat, holding up the bottle of JD.

"Suit yourself," he said. He took a long pull on the joint. "Maggie's flat. It's yours then. Really."

"No. I bought it for Maggie. It's yours now. To do with what you will."

"Why would you do that? You don't know me. You don't owe me nothing."

"I'm just a really lovely man," I said.

He laughed at that, as did I. On the floor, next to the sofa, was a mobile phone and an ancient, over-stuffed, contacts book. Dean put them on the table, then pushed them towards me. "They're yours, if you want them."

"I think I'll pass."

He ran a finger over the cover of the book. It was card, immensely worn, the corners blown, coffee and wine stains holding it all together. "It's a historical document, this." He nudged it closer to me, the joint smouldering between his fingers. "Not even a little peek?"

"No."

He sat back, relenting, tossed the book and phone onto the cushion beside him. "Hard cunt, aren't you?"

"Not really," I said. "No."

A little later I said, "Did you mean that stuff you said in the pub? About one of us killing your mum."

His gaze was not steady. He was on his third joint, his fifth bottle of Becks. The bottle of JD that I cradled in my lap was under a third full. When had I last eaten? Breakfast, perhaps. A Mars Bar. But it was a king-size one, so that was something.

"It was just bants, mate."

"Bants?"

"Well...no...just, I dunno."

"I'm not sure it matters much."

"There was something, though." It was painful, watching him try to concentrate, brow crinkling, eyes narrowed as though he could blink away the dope and the booze. "I went to see her, not long before, you know. Hadn't seen her for three, four years? But I had something to tell her. Couldn't do it, though. Chickened out. Stood outside her flat like a cunt for half an hour then just fucked off again." He opened another bottle of Becks, looked at it as though unaware of what it was then placed it carefully on the floor next to the sofa. "There was someone though. A bloke came out of mum's block. I mean, he might not have been visiting her, of course. Odds against, I suppose. Or perhaps not."

"Did you recognise him?"

"It was dark and he moved quickly and I didn't really pay him much attention. But, thinking about it, his build, the way he moved? Reminded me a bit of that prick you introduced me to."

"Ray?"

"That's it. Ray. Couldn't swear to it though."

I went to the kitchen area and rinsed out the shot glass. I took a large drink of water and placed the bottle of whisky on the work top.

When I sat again I said, "What did you want to tell your mum, Dean?"

His laugh was shrill and humourless. "Fucking gay, aren't I? I was going to come out, as though she would even give a shit."

"But you couldn't do it?"

"I don't know why not. I mean, it was pointless, but...I don't know why I couldn't do it."

"Well, you've done it now."

Another laugh, this time with a scintilla of warmth. "Yeah. Sorry. You okay with this? Stuck alone with a fucking bender?"

"I'll take my chances," I said.

We didn't make it to midnight. I left him scrabbling around for rizla papers and the rest of his dope.

"Keep in touch, yeah?" he said. I said that I would.

It was a long walk home and it was cold. At two in the morning I called Ray.

"Happy new year."

"What the fuck are you going on about?" His voice was muffled, blurred. He sounded broken.

"We need to talk," I said.

*

"Jesus," Maggie said. We were in the kitchen. The boy was in the living room, his coat still on. I could see him through the crack in the door. He was in an armchair, hunched forward, staring at his shoes. "First him, now you. I do not like surprises."

"I appreciate that you must have a very complicated diary, Maggie."

"Fuck you."

"I just thought, a little spontaneity...I even brought flowers." The bunch of daffodils lay where she had thrown them on the worktop next to the sink.

"We have an agreement."

I gave an exaggerated shrug. "I don't see anything in writing."

"You're just trying to catch me out. You bastard."

I put my hand on her shoulder. I wanted to squeeze hard, to dig my fingers into the soft flesh, but I didn't. "Perhaps I'm just trying to do a nice thing. I booked us a table at that Italian place. The one you like."

Shrugging herself away from my hand she said, "You should have called." Her voice was raised and I saw Dean's head turn toward the kitchen, heard the rustle as his cheek rubbed against the hood of his anorak.

"What are you going to do about him?" I said.

There was a tumbler full of red wine by the kettle and she took a long draught. "Go and talk to him. I'll make some calls."

Dean looked at me but didn't speak as I sat in the armchair opposite.

"Did you do that?" I said. On the coffee table was a piece of white card, folded in half, the word MUM written neatly in capital letters in red felt tip on the front of it. There was a heart as well, coloured in, and a smiley-face.

"Well, yeah," he said.

"You're right, stupid question. Who else would it be? It's good. I like it." The look he gave me would have broken my heart if I had one. "I'm not taking the piss."

"Thanks," he said. Then his head was down again, his hands together, white fingers working at the pieces of loose skin around a nail-bed. "Can I stay?"

"Your foster parents will be worried, Dean. These things need to be planned, worked out in advance."

"Why?" His eyes were liquid brown. They didn't meet mine for long and I was glad.

"It's just the way it is. How the world is. What can we do?"

He stopped picking at his fingers for a moment. "Easter then?"

"Easter," I said, standing. I could hear Maggie's voice, low and urgent, on the phone in the hallway. "Easter. Could be. Best see what the boss has to say, huh?"

He nodded slowly.

"Your foster folks? They okay?"

"Yeah. I mean...yeah. Fine."

"Good."

Then Maggie was there, a tea towel over her shoulder for no obvious reason, her mouth fixed in an odd smile. "They're on their way. They're not angry, Dean." She edged towards him as one might towards something alien. She reached a hand out towards his head and he flinched away from it. "We've got a couple of hours." It was as though she was announcing a sentence. Life. No parole.

After he'd gone she said, "Cancel the restaurant. We can eat here."

"If you say so."

"Can you go and get some wine? I've got some more calls to make."

I did as I was told.

*

We met on the bridge next to the art college. I leant on the iron railing as I waited for him, looking down river towards the next bridge, a pub. It was a new year but nobody had told the weather. The sky was all cloud, steel grey, the light flat and austere across the still water. I saw Ray walking down St Georges, past the Playhouse, hunched, hands stuffed into the familiar donkey jacket.

When he reached me I told him what Dean had said. "Was it you?"

"What if it was?"

"Three months, you said."

"So what?"

"Why lie?"

"Why not?"

"Did you hit her, Ray?"

"Did you?" He was on the balls of his feet, braced, like a bantamweight, chin jutting.

To his evident surprise and, in fact, to mine, I backed down. "You look terrible," I said. He did. Whatever protection his genetic make up had offered against years of abuse, it was clearly losing out now. His eyes were tiny, sunken, darting things. Capillaries were giving way all over his face.

"You stink of pot," he said. "What the fuck have you been up to?"

I nodded towards the Playhouse. "Bar's open. Buy me a drink and I'll tell you."

I didn't want the pint he fetched me but I drank it anyway.

"You feel sorry for him," he said after we'd caught up. "The boy?"

"Yeah. A bit."

"Didn't have him down for a fairy."

"Does it matter?"

"Apparently not. Not any more."

"Not like the good old days, hey, Ray? Bit of queer bashing. Good night out for you and the boys down the station."

"What the fuck is your problem?"

"How long have you got?" We were sat outside for some reason. There was a perfectly good, warm bar yards away but there we sat, two old men punishing ourselves.

"I mean, who the fuck are you?" I kept quiet. "Come on. With your silences and your little comments. Who are you?"

"I'm whoever you want me to be."

"Do you know exactly how creepy that sounds?" I said nothing. "Of course you do. You get off on it don't you? Other people's discomfort. Nothing touches you."

"Whatever you say."

"You patronising bastard. And you're pretty much my only friend."

"I'm not your friend, Ray."

"Jesus." He almost visibly deflated.

"I'm not your enemy either."

"Great. Cheers for that." He drained his whisky and grimaced. I reached for the glass to get another but he pushed it away and shook his head. "The answer's yes," he said.

"To what?"

"Yes, it was me. Yes, I hit her. Only once, mind. Maybe twice."

"Okay."

"I wasn't the only one. Not that that makes it any better." He turned his sunken eyes towards me. "Not you, though, of course. Not Mr Perfect."

"Not that I remember."

"Not that you remember?"

"Speaking to Dean I realised that I don't have a great grasp on the past. Timelines, stuff that happened, didn't happen."

"You'd recall something like that."

"I'd like to think so."

"There you go again. Fucking riddles."

"Why were you there, Ray? Just before she died."

"To apologise."

"Really?"

"Yeah. Really." He knuckled his eyes. He looked so old, so tired. "I mean we were finished. Done. Maggie had made that quite clear in the summer." Another look, a quick one. "Because of..." he touched the empty glass, "...well, partly this, but mostly..."

"Because you hit her?"

"Yeah. Too many men had raised their hands to her in the past, she said. I would be the last. She was very firm about it. Calm. Sure of herself. I admired her actually. Finally saw her for who she really was. Who she wanted to be at least. Not just an empty vessel. Not a just a warm body for my convenience."

"That's quite an epiphany."

"You don't believe me? Of course you don't."

"I didn't say that."

"Thing is, I'd stopped drinking for a bit. After Maggie dumped me." His face became awkward, shy. "I wanted her back. I thought it might help."

"No dice, huh?"

"I didn't even tell her. No point. She'd made her mind up. Even I could see that. Respect it even."

"So you parted on good terms."

"We did. Believe it or not. She hugged me. She was kind, actually. Kind." His eyes widened at the wonder of it. Kindness and warmth. All behind him now. Behind both of us.

"And you started drinking again."

"With both hands. I thought, why the fuck not? What difference does it make?"

*

Maggie and I had one Christmas Day together in thirty years. It was the last year of the millennium and Maggie was living in a rented house in Kentish Town. I was late but Maggie didn't seem to mind. She took the wine I'd bought, the shopping bag full of food and presents and guided me through to the small, neat living room.

The TV was on low. Some choir or other singing their hearts out. There was a woman on the sofa. I couldn't tell how old she was. Thirty? Seventy? She was bone thin with ruined hair that fell to what was left of her breasts. She was a ghost already, haunting herself, haunting us. She just didn't know it yet.

"This is Debs," Maggie said. "We were on the streets together."

"That was a while ago now, hon." Her voice was soft, blurred at the edges. There was an accent of sorts, but I couldn't place it.

"Not so long," Maggie said. "Not really."

I shook her hand. It was tiny and tremulous. "Don't worry," she said, looking into my face. "I'll be off in a minute. There's a shelter nearby does a lovely Christmas lunch. No booze, of course, but you can't have everything, am I right, hon?"

"You'll stay, Debs. Of course you will." Maggie was next to me and I felt her hip against mine. "Right?"

"Of course," I said. "The more the merrier."

But Debs was already standing, with difficulty. "Look at his face. If I stay, you'll pay and I'm not having that."

"Honestly…" I started to say but she was shuffling past me, her hand raised.

She stopped and said, "I could do with some fags though. Mebbe a drop of something to keep me warm."

I pulled a twenty out of my wallet and passed it to her. "There's a shop round the corner. It was open a minute ago."

"Paki place? I know it." She reached for the twenty then hesitated. "Can you spare another of these?" I pulled out three tenners and she took them. "Perhaps you're not so bad," she said.

"Jesus," Maggie said. "You don't have to go." She rummaged in the bag I'd brought and yanked out a couple of poorly wrapped presents and a box of Milk Tray. "Take these, at least."

"I don't think so, hon. I've got my figure to think of." She edged past us into the hallway. Maggie joined her and I watched them embrace. I could smell the turkey roasting in the kitchen. When Maggie came back into the living room she said. "Thanks for that."

"I didn't say anything."

"You didn't have to."

"She clearly wanted to go. Perhaps she's uncomfortable around men. Pretty understandable considering…"

"Considering what? You don't know the first thing about her. And what about me? Am I uncomfortable around men?"

"You seem to manage," I said.

"You bastard. You don't know the first thing about me either."

"Apparently not." I opened the wine that I'd brought into the kitchen. I couldn't see any glasses so I filled two coffee mugs and took them into the living room. Maggie was sitting at the dining table, I placed the wine in front of her. "Happy Christmas."

She took a sip and said, "You don't know what it was like."

"Of course I don't. How would I? You can tell me. If you want."

For a moment I thought she was going to but she drank some more wine instead. "Debs was the best of us."

"Really?"

"I know it's hard to believe. I didn't recognise her. First time I've seen her in, what, ten years?"

"She just turn up at the door?"

"Yeah. She saw me in the street a few days ago. Followed me here."

"That's a bit creepy."

"I expect her social skills are a bit rusty, what with the living on the street and the alcoholism and the..."

"Okay, okay. Look, you'll see her again, I'm sure."

"I don't think so." She had the cup in both hands, thumbs linked around the rim. "And, to be brutally honest, I don't want to. Which perhaps is why I was so angry. I wanted her to go. I didn't actually want her here in the first place. Looking at her..."

"What?"

"It could have been me."

"No."

"What do you know?"

"Not a lot. But that will never be you, Maggie."

I sat next to her at the table. I took one of her hands from the mug and held her fingers in mine. On the TV the choir had stopped and Noel Edmonds' face filled the screen. We couldn't hear what he was saying though so that was something.

*

He had another whiskey eventually. Of course he did. We stayed outside, in the iron cold.

"I went to see him," he said. "You know. The big fella."

"What are you talking about?"

"David. That's it. Big, smug Dave."

"David? From the funeral?"

"Who else would I be talking about?"

"What's the expression, Ray? Apropos of nothing?"

"Whatever, mate. Thing is, I know them all. I've got a list." On cue he pulled a crumpled piece of paper from his coat pocket and smoothed it out on the table. "Names and addresses. Places of employment. All of them. Even Steve."

I was curious, despite myself. I picked the paper up and skimmed it. "Why, Ray?"

"Why not? Something to do. One of the few perks of being an ex-copper. You can find stuff out."

"You're still on the case?"

He took the paper back and stuffed it into his jeans. "Not really. Not like that. Just wondered about these guys. If they had anything to hide."

"And?"

He sipped his drink then he told me about David.

His full name was David Robinson. He was a consultant structural engineer. He'd done his time with the big boys; Kier, Arup, Aecom. Worked his way up, paid his dues. Now he was freelance, cherry-picking, raking it in. He had a detached house on Newmarket Road. He drove a BMW, his wife an Audi. Or was it the other way round? His son was months away from qualifying as a GP, his daughter was on a gap year, travelling.

Ray followed him on and off for a week then

cornered him in Roger Hickman's restaurant in St Giles. He was eating at a corner table with his wife. Ray waited outside for ten minutes then slipped in, straight past the small bar and said, "Dave. Long time no see."

He enjoyed the look on David's face, fork, laden with salad and salmon, stalled halfway to his mouth. His wife, predictably gorgeous and immaculate, placed a hand gently on her husband's arm and said, "David?"

The bigger man recovered. He put his fork down and stood, extending his hand. "Ray. Look, not a great time, as you can see." He passed Ray a business card. "Call me. We'll have a coffee."

A waiter was approaching. "Yeah, bit rude, I suppose, thinking about it. I'll ring." To the waiter, "I'm going, I'm going. Great to meet you, Meg."

"You too," David's wife said. Bewildered and wary but still polite.

Three days later they met in a Starbucks in the city centre. Ray was there first, David made an entrance, hurling his coat onto the seat opposite Ray, "What the hell was that all about?"

"Sit down, David. I'll get us a coffee."

"I don't want a coffee. This won't take long."

"We'll see. And you might as well have one. I am."

David sighed and sat. "Flat white. Decaf."

"Rock and roll," Ray said.

When he returned, Ray continued. "Hey, I was passing, saw you through the window. Couldn't pass up the opportunity of saying hi to an old friend."

"Spare me, please. What do you want? I'm a busy man."

"I'm sure you are. Big house, flash cars."

David shrugged. "What's your point? I've done

well for myself. Everything I have I've worked hard for. It's no less than I deserve."

"Bit defensive, Dave, but I'm sure that's true. How about Meg? The lovely Meg. What does she deserve exactly?"

His face reddening, David said, "That's enough. What's this? Blackmail? I won't..."

"Easy. Easy. I'm just messing with you, mate. I just want to talk, that's all. No threats. Not really." Lunchtime was approaching and the tables around them were filling up. "What did you tell her? After I left?"

"I said you were an old acquaintance. From Uni."

"You flatter me."

"Indeed I do. Sounds better than washed up ex-policeman. Not to mention the drinking."

"Touché." He sipped his latte. It was weak, lukewarm. "Thing is, we do have something in common."

David sat back, more relaxed now, raising a single finger in front of his face, like an umpire confirming a dismissal. "One thing. That's hardly the basis for..."

"I look at your life, David, your lovely, lovely life and I can't see how Maggie fitted in. You were slumming it, presumably."

"That really is absolutely none of your business."

"Well, of course it isn't. Be no fun if it was. But I'm just a washed up old copper with too much time on my hands and nothing whatever to lose. Not to mention the drinking. It can make me very unpredictable."

"So it's threats again?"

"I am an easy man to humour. So just humour me, David and I'll go away."

David nodded slightly and drained his coffee. When he spoke his voice was rich and controlled and even. "I wasn't slumming it, as you so charmingly put it.

Not in the slightest. I can see why you might think that...but, no. Not at all."

"Good."

"I was at a conference, about three years ago. Structural engineering thing. Massive do at a hotel in Birmingham. Deathly dull, as you can imagine. It was a big hotel, it was hosting about four separate events that night and there was an enormous communal bar in the centre. Waifs and strays from the various do's gathered there. It was a change of air, I suppose. Of company. It was late, I'd had enough of engineers for one evening. Or for many evenings, if I'm honest. So one drink and bed, that was the plan."

"And there she was."

"Yes. There she was. She was at the bar, I was at the bar. She wore a simple black dress. A velvety thing. Black choker. She had her hair up. She looked..."

"I know how she looked."

"Yes. Of course." His demeanour had changed, softened. "She'd been stood up, she said. I told her I found that hard to believe. I bought her a drink."

"And one thing led to another."

"The thing I regret...I mean really regret...is in the morning I offered her money."

"You charmer. But she forgave you."

"She was the forgiving sort, wasn't she? Maggie."

"Up to a point," Ray said. Then at David's querying look. "Nothing. Carry on."

"I..." He toyed with his coffee cup. "Look, this wasn't me. I'd never..."

"You're probably explaining to the wrong person, Dave."

"I'm not a risk taker. I value what I have. What Meg and I have. The kids, everything..." His voice tailed off again.

"I've been there, mate. She gets under your skin."

"Yes. She does. Did. She was like a drug. No excuse, of course, but..."

"And you kept it quiet? For three years?"

"I travel a lot and Meg is very trusting. She never had any reason not to be. And it's not as though we got together that often. Not often enough, is how it seems now. Maggie was very discrete. In her line of business, I suppose you have to be."

"Her line of business?"

"Counselling. Couples therapy."

"I see."

"What?"

"Nothing. Why did you go to the funeral? That was a risk wasn't it?"

"Yes. It was. It was stupid and reckless but I couldn't not go. It's not as though I know anyone in Mendham."

"Still, you wouldn't have me to worry about if you hadn't gone."

"That is a very good point." He reached for his coat. "I think that's enough, Ray. I've been very frank. I think you have enough decency about you to keep this to yourself."

"Again with the flattery." David stood. "One last question," Ray said.

"He last saw her a month before she died," Ray said. "Meg had a weekend away with the girls so he and Maggie rented a cottage on the North Norfolk coast. Brancaster, I think it was."

"Right."

"What?"

"Nothing. You believe him?"

"Yeah. I actually think it was good for him. Talking about it. Cathartic? Is that the word?"

"So you were doing him a favour?"

"You could say that."

"Did you ask if she was drinking?"

"I did. She wasn't. And they didn't fuck either."

"He *was* frank."

"Well, he didn't put it like that, not big, posh Dave. But...they hadn't much...recently. It mattered to him that I knew. It wasn't all about the sex. Not in the end."

"Did you buy that?"

"Why not. If we're being honest here it was the same for me." He waited a beat. "You?"

"Honesty is overrated."

"Perhaps. Still. I've shared. Your turn."

"It hadn't been physical for a while. It didn't matter."

"Whatever good old Cyth said, it wasn't all about the sex."

"Apparently not. So what was it about?"

"Fucked if I know."

I drained my pint. "Would you have told his wife?"

"Sure. Why not? Still might." I looked at him and he shrugged. "I never said I wasn't a cunt."

*

We met in a coffee shop, all those years ago. It was in Norwich, Elm Hill, the cobbles slick with fresh rain. It was early summer and the shower passed quickly. The air was rich with it, though, ripe and swollen.

She was in the corner, on her own, a pot of tea and a copy of The Guardian in front of her. She wore a light raspberry-coloured sweater and faded jeans. Her hair was blonde, shoulder-length, shot through with sunlight from the window behind her.

She didn't look up when I entered. I took a coffee and nursed it in the corner. I was hungover. I kept looking at her and she met my eyes once, gave a tight smile and went back to her paper.

Eventually I paid for another coffee and went over to her table and asked if I could join her. She folded her paper in half while she considered. "Look," she said. "I've been stood up."

"I'm sorry," I said, yanking a chair out and sitting opposite her.

"That wasn't an invitation," she said. Her eyes were stern but I didn't buy it.

"I know," I said. "Don't mind me, I'm just sitting here, drinking my coffee."

"Okay." A soft mouth, white teeth.

"I've got a hangover," I said.

"Me too, as it happens."

"You're hiding it well."

"Thanks. You're not."

"Open book, me." I held out my hand and she shook it quickly. I told her my name and she told me hers.

"I like dancing," she said.

"Me too."

"Really?"

"Love it."

"Really?"

"No. Not at all. Several left feet. But never too late to learn, right?"

"Right." She examined her tea cup and found it to be empty. "You should know, there is someone."

"Well, yeah. The guy who stood you up."

Her eyes became luminous. "There is someone."

"There's always someone," I said.

*

Ray left. The day wound down. A week later I bumped into Zack.

I knew from Ray's list that he lived in the flats at the end of St Benedicts. He was staring into the window of the Cash Converters when I saw him. It was a Tuesday afternoon, mild and still. I offered my hand and he took it before he recognised me. Then he grinned and hugged me, which I didn't expect. The Plasterers Arms was nearby. "My local," he said. He ordered a rum, neat, apologising for the stereotype. We shed our jackets and sat on stools at a blond wood table.

"I felt bad about leaving so quickly after the funeral," he said. "Leaving you with the boy."

"It's fine. He wasn't so bad."

"Good. Still, I'm glad to see you. To apologise. It didn't sit right with me."

I shrugged it off and he took the hint and changed the subject. He was pleasant, enquiring and interested, which was endearing and irritating in equal measure. I dead batted his questions about me for a bit then turned the focus onto him.

"We came over from Jamaica in the fifties. London. Didn't settle. I washed up here twenty, thirty years ago?" He paused as he checked the numbers. "Who am I kidding? Nearer forty." He stretched out his right hand, considered the liver spots spreading there. "How did this happen?" He sighed. "I am a simple man. Happy, mostly. Give me a roof over my head, a little money, some company..." His breath deepened. "But sometimes you dwell. There's too much past. Too many things you won't get to do." He smiled as he looked at me. It was a good smile. Warm. "You know, I don't think I'm ever going to open the bowling for the West Indies."

"Have you seen them lately? Don't give up hope just yet."

A deep laugh to match the smile. "It's true, it's true. But it wasn't always that way. I was at the Oval when Mikey Holding tore though you guys."

"1976? Whispering Death. He's a Jamaican, isn't he?"

An approving nod. "He's a great man. I met him once, in the bar after a county game. We spoke for an hour and he shook my hand."

"Pace like fire."

"Yes. Pace like fire. There's the past again. Looming up, taking big chunks of us."

"It's cricket, it's fine."

"There are worse places to lose yourself." His glass was empty. He looked at it as though he wasn't sure how that had happened. I offered to get him another but he shook his head. "I think we were through, Maggie and I. Had been for a while."

"I'd been getting that feeling myself."

"But I miss her. It was only a couple of years and our meetings were...infrequent. But still." He picked up his empty glass, put it down again. "Do you mind me talking like this?"

"Not at all."

"It was mostly physical, is what I'm trying to say. I mean, there was a connection, but it was mostly..." His voice tailed off.

"I understand."

"You do? Then you are a better man than I. The last few times it wasn't even that. I don't know what it was. Two lost souls clinging to each other amidst the wreckage perhaps."

"You don't seem like a lost soul."

"That's good." He was wearing a short-sleeved shirt and he ran a hand over the skin of a bare forearm. "She got under here." He raised a fist to his chest. "And in here. I don't know how. It's like an infection. I am not a faithful man. I've never pretended to be." He had drifted a little but now he focussed again, looked into my face. "That foolish guy? At the funeral? Steve, I think. It's not us who should get tested. It was Maggie."

"Oh, she did."

"Good. We are none of us faithful men, I think."

"Probably not. Did she drink around you, Zack?"

"Not for a while. Not that I can remember. But we're talking an hour in a hotel room. An afternoon at my place. We didn't socialise much. Look, perhaps I will have another drink."

It was mid afternoon and the pub was how I liked it, almost empty. The girl behind the bar was pretty and vacant and I thought of the Sex Pistols song as she took my order.

When I passed him his rum he said, "Do you read?"

"Some. Not enough, I suppose."

"I love it. Can't get enough. I like fiction, but anything will do. I must be a writer's dream. I don't care about the quality, the prose, the...vocabulary." He stretched the word out. "I eat it all up. I don't travel now, not for a few years." He rubbed his fingers together. "Lack of funds, you know? But with a book you can go anywhere. Anytime. And the library is free. For now. The wonder of it."

"Maggie was a reader."

"She turned me onto some good stuff. Sallis.

Salter. Chester Himes. We talked about books. Towards the end that's pretty much all we did." I felt a stab of jealousy. All the times Maggie sat lost in a paperback, how often had I asked her what she was reading, how she felt about it? Once, twice, in thirty years? "I learnt stuff from that girl," Zack said. "What did I ever teach her, huh?"

"She didn't need teaching, Zack."

"Sure she did. We all do."

I tried to turn the talk back to cricket but his good nature was worn away by the rum and the memories. We parted with a handshake. "The hand that shook Michael Holdings hand," I said.

"That's something," he said.

"It is." He raised an arm as he left, just as he had after Maggie's funeral.

"Sounds like a nice guy," Ray said. Another January afternoon. We were on a bench in Eaton Park.

"He is." We could see the boating lake from where we sat. It was empty, the water raked with stiff, chilled ripples.

Ray held his hands out in front of him. They shook uncontrollably. "Shit," he said.

"How long?"

"Less than a day. I'm fucked, man."

"Your choice, you said. Whatever happens."

"As ever, such a comfort."

"If you go cold turkey for much longer you're going to crash. Black outs, DT's, it's a hard road."

"You speaking from experience?"

"My dad, as it happens."

"Right. Sorry. But there's no half measures with the 12 step guys. You don't drink. That's it."

"I know. A day at a time. You going to AA?"

"Not exactly. Trying to do it on my own. It's worked before. More or less. For a while, at least."

To our left the last group of parents and kids left the play area. The roundabout still turned mournfully, a swing creaked. Ray's face was grey, his eyes sunken.

"I found Steve," he said.

"Okay."

"It's something to do. Turns out he is not a nice man."

"The clues were there."

"He's a builder. Lives up Thorpe way. I followed him to work a couple of days ago."

"How did that turn out?"

"He wasn't happy. It took him a minute to clock who I was. Then...well, he swore a lot."

"Pot and kettle?"

"Perhaps. But...she was a slag, was the theme. Maggie. A fucking slag and variations thereof, over and over. We were welcome to her. Druggie, whore, fucking slapper..."

"I get it, Ray."

"Yeah. I got it too but he didn't stop. I tried to hit him, mate." Some colour leached into his cheeks. "Wasn't up to it, was I? He slapped me off like I was a fly. Cunt."

I tried to remember Steve: wiry, feral. Ray had an edge to him too but it was blunted by drink. "Nothing to be ashamed of, Ray."

"You think? You really think?" His voice shook. "He said he was showering four times a day but he still couldn't wash away the stink of her."

I took a long breath. "He could have killed her then."

"No. I mean, yes, he was capable. But, no. I checked. He was in Norwich when Maggie died.

Working, then in the pub. That's about the only good thing I can say for him. He didn't kill her."

After he left I sat there for a while as the light drained and the cold settled around my shoulders. Later I went to a corner shop and then to his flat.

"You again. I'm honoured." His face was paper-white, beaded with sweat.

I thrust a bottle of Jamesons at him. "Drink some of this."

"Seriously? I'm crawling up the walls here and you bring me this?"

"You can't take it, Ray. It's as simple as that."

The bottle hung between us. Then he took it, twisted the top off and took a long draught. "Bastard," he said. I wasn't sure whether he was talking to me or the whisky.

I sat at his kitchen table while he took a shower. There were papers scattered over the table; hand-written notes, computer print outs, some images. They were in no order. I flicked through a few idly, then something drew my attention.

Ray was rubbing his hair dry when he entered the kitchen.

"You seen this?" I said, handing him some A4 sheets.

"I've not been through all these. Bit distracted." He took the paper and read for a moment. "Jesus," he said.

"Well, yes," I said.

*

We met outside Samantha's on a warm Friday night. She wore tight jeans and a thin lemon-coloured top that stopped just below her navel. Her arms were bare. Her hair was a dirty blonde and fell to her shoulders.

"You look good," I said.

"You too." Her scent was rich as she kissed my cheek. I followed her up the narrow stairs into the club.

In those days you knew early on if you were in for a good evening at Samantha's. Marley was playing when we entered, the bass enormous and visceral, sucking us in. The floor was packed but mellow. She took my hand and pulled me into the throng. No drinks at first, although we made up for it later.

She hit the rhythm instantly. Or it took her perhaps. I don't know what I did. It didn't matter. They played *Walk On By*, the original and then the Stranglers' version, back to back. When the Stranglers came on there were a few seconds respite and Maggie's eyes met mine and her smile was small and querulous. Then the bass came in, like a detonation, and she was gone. It was relentless, driving through walls, hammering through all of us but she took it easily, arms raised above her head, hips twisting, sweat gathering on her face and throat. Her face was tilted upwards, eyes closed, lips parted. It was as though she was approaching orgasm. Perhaps she was.

Later, at hers, she said, "A couple of things."

"Okay." I kissed the sweat from her throat.

"Seriously," she said, pushing me back.

"Okay," I said. I put my hands in my lap.

It wasn't full disclosure. It never was with Maggie. Perhaps that's a bit rich coming from me.

She told me about the drugs and about her years on the game. She said she was chaotic, unreliable, perhaps a little bit broken. Men thought they could fix her, she said. They couldn't. She didn't want them to. When she finished her eyes were wide. I nodded.

"It's fine," I said. I was eager for what was to come. "It's all fine."

Her head dipped. Before it did, it's possible that I caught the merest hint of disappointment on her face. Then she reached for me.

*

Phil was a lecturer in Religious Studies at the UEA. He had a class on Wednesday afternoons and Ray and I waited for him at the bottom of some steps outside a concrete block of a building. The low winter sun caught his glasses as he adjusted them, pausing, when he saw us.

"Hey," Ray said.

"What's this?" Phil said, as he joined us. A mild, ascetic face. Soft eyes. A smile of sorts.

"You rushed off after the funeral," I said.

"Well...I'm sorry. I didn't mean to appear rude." He spread his hands, Adam's apple bobbing. "Busy, busy, You know how it is." A glance at his watch. "Actually, guys, I've got another class..."

"No you don't," Ray said. "You're done for the day. Tough life, huh?" He put his hand on Phil's arm.

"We need to grab a coffee, Phil. Have a chat."

"I don't think..."

"Yeah, we do. Unless you fancy something stronger?"

"It's a bit early for me," Phil said.

"Figured as much," I said. "Where's the canteen?" He nodded past Ray's left shoulder. "Good man," I said.

The canteen was large and sterile and almost empty. We sat in a corner. Ray fetched the coffees, which were weak and insipid. It didn't matter. None of us cared about the coffee.

When we'd settled I said, "How long have you known Cynthia?"

"Who?"

"Cynthia Kemp."

"I have no idea..." His Adam's apple was frantic now. He pushed his glasses up to the bridge of his nose.

"You are not a good liar, Phil," Ray said. "Give it up."

"The Friends of Mendham Church have a meeting every month," I said. "Hosted by our Cynth. You've been the guest speaker, more than once. It's on the Internet, it must be true. And you live in Mendham, don't you? Mendham church is your church. It would be impossible for you not to know Cynthia Kemp."

"What if I..."

"And there's the photos, of course," Ray said.

"Photos?"

"Local press. Church website. Fund raisers, bake sales, church fête. All with you and Cynthia, thick as thieves."

"Well, it's not a crime, is it?"

"Why lie about it?"

"Why not? Quite frankly, none of this is any of your business."

We were sat either side of him, hemming him in. "Sure it is," I said. "That little act at the funeral? Pretty good. Perhaps you can lie. Thing is, Phil, if you knew Cynthia you knew about us. All of us."

"What if I did?"

"Why pretend that you didn't?" Ray said. "What was the point of that?"

"Perhaps I was ashamed."

"No," I said. "That's not it. Come on, Phil. Confession is good for the soul. You of all people should know that."

"That's not quite my denomination," Phil said. Ray laughed. Phil sighed and laid his hands flat on the table. His fingers were long and pale and thin. "I met Maggie through the church. About a year ago. It was a while before Cynthia got her claws into her."

"That's no way to speak about a friend," I said.

"I used to think she meant well. She was brusque, rude, even, but that was just her way. But I thought she had God in her heart. I believed she was doing his work."

"And now?"

He waited a beat. "Perhaps she thinks that she is. If one is being kind."

"Which you try to be, Phil, I'm sure."

He turned to me, his eyes pale and guileless. "I like to think so."

"Anyway," Ray said. "Maggie."

Phil's hands went to his glasses, his face. "Maggie," he said. "I've lead an academic life. A dry life, in many ways. Controlled, self contained. It's entirely deliberate and I've always been quite happy. I'm not attempting to elicit any sympathy."

"I don't think we're going to start feeling sorry for you, Phil," Ray said.

"Quite. Good." He pushed his spectacles back again, to the top of his nose. "She latched onto me and I was flattered. We talked about God, about belief. Over coffee, lunch. She was intelligent and engaged and interested. It was...enervating."

"You fancied her," Ray said.

"I found her attractive, certainly. I didn't expect that to be reciprocated but it turns out that it was. We started...dating. Meals mostly, the cinema. Theatre. I would like to have seen her more often but she was busy she said and I had no reason to doubt her." He became awkward. "After a couple of months or so I asked her to marry me. She said yes."

Ray and I looked at each other and then back at Phil.

"I was as surprised as you two obviously are. But I was delighted too." He looked at his lap. "No fool like an old fool."

"Had you set a date?" I said.

"No. It wasn't long after that that Cynthia got involved. She didn't know about Maggie and I. I don't know why I kept it from her. Cynthia and I were friends, after all. Instinct, perhaps."

"What happened?"

"What always happens with Cynthia. She took Maggie under her wing. It only took her so long because she had another girl to whose spiritual needs she was attending. When that one drifted away she turned her attentions to Maggie. She took her away from me in many ways."

"Did she really?" I said, as gently as I could.

He nodded eagerly. "I think so. Maggie was...reinventing herself. And it was working. I didn't need to know...anything. I didn't care. But once one knows, one can't...not know."

"She told Cynthia about us, about her past. But not you. Why?"

"Have you met Cynthia?" he said. We nodded. "Then you know. But at first she would have been warm and charming." He saw our faces and said, "I know, but it's true. Especially with women. The lost and vulnerable. She can sense it. And Maggie was open, so keen to learn. They became inseparable. Maggie would have trusted her."

"That doesn't sound like Maggie," I said.

"Well, she *was* lost, she *was* vulnerable. She

wanted to trust. She just chose the wrong person, that's all."

"It should have been you," Ray said.

Phil said nothing. A waif of a girl dressed in a navy blue overall was clearing the tables around us and we waited until she had finished. "I was jealous of Cynthia. Not you two. Not the other guys."

"But she told you about us?"

"Of course she did. Couldn't wait. I remember the relish on her face. It shocked me. It shocks me still. I sometimes wonder if Cynthia's God is my God."

"I didn't know you got to choose your God, Phil," Ray said quietly. I looked at him, surprised.

"With respect, that isn't quite what I said. You probably don't want to be arguing religious semantics with a theology lecturer." Ray bristled at that a little but let it go. I watched him compose himself as he let Phil continue. "I ended it with Maggie. It broke my heart but it had to be done."

"It did?"

He sighed. "It wasn't...shame. Or jealousy. It wasn't physical at all. We were Christians, we were saving ourselves until we were married."

"You were?" I said.

"Of course."

"Of course," Ray said.

"Then why?" I said. "If you loved her so much."

He became uncomfortable. "My reputation. That's the truth of it. The church. My position here. And my father is still alive."

"Jesus," I said.

"It's almost a toss up between you and Steve," Ray said.

"What?" Phil said.

"Nothing."

"How did she take it?" I said.

"Better than I deserved. She was noble, resigned. It br..."

"Don't say it broke your heart," Ray said, standing suddenly, his back to us, hands clenched.

"Okay," Phil said. He looked at me uncertainly, I shrugged. "She felt betrayed by Cynthia. I know that much. Understandably, I suppose."

"I suspect she felt betrayed a lot," I said. "Over the years."

"I wouldn't know about that," Phil said.

"No, you wouldn't," Ray said, sitting again. "I still don't get why you lied. At the funeral. You fucking milksop."

"Honestly," Phil said, "there's no need..."

"Shut up," Ray said. His voice was not raised but there was a steel tone I hadn't heard before. "Why did you lie? We didn't care what you knew, what you didn't know."

He absorbed the silence that followed, two sets of eyes on him. "You can't believe..." His long fingers fluttered in front of him. "I wouldn't...I couldn't do that."

"Actually," Ray said, "I think that you could." Phil started to protest but Ray raised a hand, stilling him. "But I don't think you did."

"So why did you lie?" I said.

His pale cheeks reddened. "I am still loyal. To the church. To Cynthia."

"Cynthia?"

"I mean...it was natural causes, I know. Nothing suspicious. But still. No point stirring things up."

"You think Cynthia killed Maggie?"

He turned his pale, mild eyes towards Ray. "To paraphrase your friend here, I don't think she did kill her. But I think that she could."

Nobody spoke for a while. Phil gingerly extricated himself from his corner seat and edged passed Ray as one would pass something feral. We didn't stop him and he walked away without a backward glance.

Ray and I found the student bar. We were so painfully out of place it was almost funny.

"I used to drink here," I said. "Back in the day. It's changed."

"Or perhaps you have," Ray said.

"Deep."

He grunted. We were served by someone with piercings and ornate facial hair. He still looked thirteen years old, fourteen tops. We found a corner. It wasn't dark enough. It felt as though we were surrounded by children pretending to be adults. Or perhaps it was the other way round.

"That Phil, quite a prince, huh?"

"I don't know," I said. "Perhaps he was the one. If Cynthia hadn't intervened."

"You think? Phil and Maggie walking down the aisle? It'd be an interesting wedding night."

"She was shutting the rest of us down. One by one."

"Even you?"

"Even me. Slowly, but still. She was letting me go. I was the last of us, I suppose."

"First in, last out."

"Fairs fair. I'd put the years in after all."

"Such bitterness doesn't suit you." He drank some whisky, grimaced. "Scratch that. Of course it fucking does."

I sipped my own drink without tasting it. We had become invisible now, amongst the hum of young voices. Usually I like being invisible. But not now. "I can't stand this," I said.

We drained our glasses and left.

It was a long walk back into the city centre and we didn't talk much.

Eventually Ray said, "She just died then."

"Looks that way."

"I'm not sure I even care any more."

"You keep telling yourself that," I said.

"I think, after all, that Maggie was just another addiction."

I looked at him as we walked and said nothing.

For a couple of weeks after that I followed Steve around. Covertly, from a distance. We all have our habits and Steve's were easier to discern that most. He was working on an extension to a terraced house off Mousehold Heath. Four evenings a week he visited the Quebec pub. Fridays and Saturdays he stayed until they kicked him out, at around midnight. He walked home alone, talking a shortcut through Lion Wood.

On the third Friday in February, just after Valentine's Day, I followed him as he walked home. It was raining. He was very drunk. He entered the woods, staggering slightly, oblivious. I had a cosh. I'd made it myself years ago. I came up behind him and snapped it twice across the back of his head. He went straight down, boneless. I looked at him for a moment. Rain soaked into his jeans and jacket, rinsed the blood from his thin, fair hair. I kicked him in the kidneys and lower back. I walked around him. I broke a rib or two. I heard something go in his nose. It occurred to me that I didn't have to stop. I could keep punching and kicking. But I did stop. I don't know why. It wasn't pity. Perhaps I was tired. I left him in the rain and the mud and his own blood and walked home.

*

It was a Friday in autumn, the last time I saw Maggie. We had lunch at a new coffee shop on Riverside. Our conversation consisted of the many shortcuts we had accumulated over the years. No new neural pathways here, just the old familiar routes. There was comfort in it. Her salad was fine, she said. My sandwich was dry. The coffee was mediocre. We won't come back, she said. We didn't.

We took a walk later, a long one, taking in a chunk of Marriotts way. The air was soft and warm, the light golden and yielding. She took my hand for a while at one point then let it drop again. I remember thinking then, we are frozen here. We have calcified. But did I really think that or have I added it later? The sublime luxury of hindsight. Memories shift.

We saw a play later at the Maddermarket Theatre. A friend of one of Maggie's former friends was the female lead. She wasn't very good and neither was the play.

Later, at hers, she said, did I mind not staying? She had an early start.

No problem, l said and asked about Sunday.

She was going to church she said and I laughed. It had become a standing joke. At least that's what I thought it was.

It would be tempting to think I had some sort of premonition when we said goodbye. I didn't. We hugged and she kissed my cheek. I was a little annoyed about Sunday so I didn't kiss her back. Did her hair smell of peaches? Probably. It usually did. When the door closed I felt what I always felt. Regret. Relief.

*

By late Spring Dean had sorted out the paperwork and settled into Maggie's old flat. I visited him on a sultry Wednesday in May. The door was answered by a thickset man in his thirties. He wore a Steely Dan t-shirt with knee-length shorts and a pork pie hat. He had a full beard that twitched at the edges when he smiled. Which he did when he saw me. Dean was behind him suddenly, a tea towel in his hand.

"This is Gavin," he said. Gavin nodded. "He's staying for a while." Gavin's head tilted to one side at that, as did his beard. "Make us some tea, Gav," Dean said. Gav did.

"I like what you've done with the place," I said as I entered and this time I meant it. The walls were freshly painted in muted shades. The floors were bare mostly, some rugs here and there. There was lots of naked, pale wood. The lighting had dimmer switches. There were some lamps dotted around, a sprinkling of cool, understated prints.

"This is all Gavin," Dean said. "It's nice enough, I suppose."

"So," I said, "You and Gavin..."

Dean rolled his eyes. "Give me a break, granddad."

"Whatever," I said.

We drank tea in the warm, clean living room. Gavin barely spoke yet still managed to exude niceness and calm. Dean talked about his mum a bit and I nodded in the right places. Gavin placed his hand on Dean's arm at one point, lightly, then withdrew it again.

Dean was out of the motor trade. He and Gavin were hoping to open a coffee shop in Mendham. They had their eyes on a vacant property. Gavin had some cash and there was the equity in the flat, of course.

When Dean popped to the bathroom Gavin said, "I heard what you did. The flat. That's cool, man."

"Plenty you haven't heard," I said.

He nodded sagely. "Yeah. Ain't it always so."

"Can't argue with that," I said.

As I left Gavin was cleaning up in the kitchen. "No dope?" I said.

"Gavin doesn't like it," Dean said.

"He's a good influence. I approve."

"Fuck you," Dean said, but he was laughing and he hugged me at the door. "Keep in touch. Come round for a meal sometime. Gavin's a great cook."

"Of course he is," I said.

The sun was warm and bright when I left Dean's. I made my way to the church, to visit Maggie's grave, but Cynthia had beaten me to it. She was kneeling there, patting fussily at an arrangement of daffodils and crocuses. The oak tree across from us was in bloom. Wild flowers were dotted between the graves. Their scent was rich and heady. An early, exploratory bee bumbled gingerly from one to another.

"I'm the only one who leaves flowers," she said without turning, without looking at me. "The only one who visits. Every day..."

"Don't give me that, Cynthia. It's not everyday. Not by any means."

She turned at that. "How would you know?" Her glasses glittered in the sunlight and I couldn't see her eyes. "Have you been following me?"

"I know," I said. "I mean, fair play, you're here more than me, more than the rest of them. But cut the bullshit."

"Honestly. There's no need for..."

"I said cut it, Cynthia."

She stood with difficulty. She had on a plain white t-shirt and a long linen skirt. The cross she wore swung on her chest as she stood. "You can't threaten me."

"I can. Actually. Feel free to ignore me. Most people do. How's Phil? It's nice to see that you're friends again."

She folded her arms across her chest. "He's a fool. But he's our fool, I suppose. I know you talked."

"I don't doubt it. Were you jealous? Was that it?"

Her bewilderment seemed genuine. "Jealous? Of Maggie? Because of Phil?"

"She kept her looks, didn't she? Despite everything." I thought of Ray and his good genes. "I don't know how. But she was radiant. Beautiful. Were you ever beautiful, Cynthia?"

"You think I'm that shallow? Do not judge me by your own standards, Mr..."

"We're all the same deep down. You can hide behind your God all you like. She rejected you in the end. They all did. All your pretty girls."

"They needed me. I helped them. I helped Maggie."

"Yeah. You helped her. You helped her good."

She took off her glasses and cleaned them slowly. "Do you know what she said about you?"

"I think I can..."

"You were hollow, she said. Blank. Just a good looking void. Her precise words."

"Thirty years," I said.

"She was a people pleaser," Cynthia spat. "She was whatever you wanted her to be. Whatever Ray wanted. All of you..."

"And you, Cynthia."

"What?"

"I think you're right, for what it's worth. But it was the same with you. The faith, the belief, she sucked you in too. Until you stabbed her in the back, of course."

"She was a harlot. A whore. I could have saved her. I could have saved all of them."

"All of them," I said. "All your lost girls. We wondered, Ray and I, how many of them died before their time."

"It was Maggie's time."

"He's looking into it. Ray." This wasn't entirely true. What Ray was mostly doing was drinking himself to death. "He has the time, the contacts and he doesn't like you much." Her head tilted towards me. She squinted in the bright light. I thought of Phil's eyes. Pale and moist. Nothing much there. "Did you kill her, Cynthia?"

She seemed to come to her senses. She steadied herself as she put her glasses back on. She checked the graveyard and the street beyond the low stone wall. There was nobody around but us.

"I could have done," she said quietly. I had to lean forward to hear her. "Could easily have done. She was so soundly asleep, you see. And she looked so innocent, at peace." Suddenly she was no longer squinting. She reached out a hand. "Give me your phone."

"What?"

"They can records things these days."

"I'm not recording..." I sighed and pulled out my old Nokia. "Satisfied?"

She took it from me and fiddled with it until it was turned off. She dropped it into the grass next to Maggie's grave. "Perhaps she wasn't already dead," she said. She was looking past me now, past the oak tree, past everything. "I could have put my fingers to her nose, pinched her nostrils together. Gently, of course. My other hand would have gone across her mouth, had things happened this way. The probability is that she was already dead. She would have struggled, surely, had she been alive."

"You witch," I said.

"Perhaps God was there. With me. With her. He took her last breath. It's possible that I helped. It's possible that I didn't."

Her eyes came back to mine. They were entirely empty. A dog barked somewhere and another answered. The air was cooling as the afternoon ran down.

*

We were walking once, at Reedham, on the edge of the broad. It was Spring then too, the light golden across the wetlands. We came across a swan's nest, just off a main path. It was mostly surrounded by reeds but we could see the pen, her head turning towards us. We watched for a moment from a respectful distance.

Maggie whispered, "A few years ago I'd have rushed up to her, tried to hug her or something."

"They can break a man's arm. So they say."

"That wouldn't have stopped me. I'd have tried, at least. Fool that I was."

"And now?"

"I'm still a fool, but less so, I think." She looked at me and I shrugged, non-committal. "Well, thanks," she said.

"Just joshing."

"Hilarious. I don't need your validation. I remember. Every day a fresh apocalypse."

I miss it, I nearly said, but didn't. "Do you remember the warning you gave me on our first evening together?" She shook her head. I recited it, word for word.

"The romance," she said.

"I'm still here." I laid my hand on her waist and she moved against me. We watched the swan for a while. It stared back at us without concern.

*

Ray's hanging in there. Maintenance drinking, he calls it, but it's a little more than that. We meet up from time to time. He talks about Maggie for a bit then he passes out and I leave. It's a pattern we've fallen into. It won't last forever but, oddly, I'll miss it when it ends.

Dean and Gavin opened their coffee shop. I was there on the first day. It was...interesting. I'm not sure Mendham is ready for Gavin. I give the venture six months, a year. Dean and Gavin, however, could be in it for the long haul. I find that I'm pleased.

I saw Zack once, in the city centre. We were yards from each other. He hesitated, we both did. Then he half grinned, raised an arm and kept on walking. So did I.

Phil took early retirement and moved to Devon. I know where he lives. I know where Cynthia lives too, of course. She's still in Mendham, although she no longer visits Maggie's grave. I think of her and Phil from time to time. Long thoughts. I have time on my hands and nothing much to lose.

Walk On By plays on the stereo. The Stranglers' version. I turn the volume right up and when the bass comes in it's as though Maggie's there, arms raised, head thrown back, hips twisting, lost in the music. I can see her navel as her blouse rides up. I can smell her scent. I can see the sweat in her hair and on her throat.

Sour Times

Carter waited for Janice in a half empty bar on Riverside on a warm Wednesday evening in late spring. A scattering of couples and groups of office workers were sitting outside on the large terrace that abutted the river. Carter nursed his Peroni in a corner seat. They had arranged to meet inside the bar and, anyway, Carter preferred corners and niches and hints of shadow, always had. Something by Portishead played in the background.

It was almost eight when she came through the double doors and he knew at once. It wasn't how she looked. She still exuded that sense of compact, self-contained prettiness that had initially attracted him. Her hair was up, she wore a hint of make-up, just enough. Her dress was crisp and summery and apt. Instead it was the odd angle of her smile and the cast of her eyes that gave it away and Carter wondered if she saw the same expression reflected back at her.

Sometimes things just don't work out. No reason in particular, nobody to blame. An acquaintance of Carter's had once told him that mathematics explained everything. It all fitted, he said, there was an equation for every transaction, crisp and perfect and beyond reproach. If that were the case, Carter thought, then the numbers generated by he and Janice didn't quite add up. They were a fraction out. A decimal point, perhaps. Their calculations didn't mesh.

Carter ordered a chilled white wine for Janice and they sat opposite each other and observed the necessary protocols. Carter could not recall much in the way of detail from their previous dates – viewing a light romcom together at Cinema City, sharing a pizza at the new place near the market – but he was sure that the conversation had flowed easily and there had been little or no awkwardness between them. Now they were trapped behind a wall of politeness. Janice was a nurse, so Carter asked her about her day and she told him. Then she reciprocated and Carter shrugged. Carter's work was a source of concern even when things were going well in a relationship. To the inevitable question, "So what do you do?" Carter had, over the years, tried a variety of responses:

"Import, export."

"Freelance troubleshooter."

Carter's favourite fictional character, Matt Scudder, had replied to this question by saying that he did "favours for friends". Carter had tried this once. Turns out that what sounds cool in a made up story about a burnt out PI in Hell's Kitchen, becomes borderline creepy when transposed to a *Wetherspoons* in Norwich city centre. Who knew?

After half an hour Janice sat back in her seat and puffed out her cheeks. Her wine was untouched.

"It's fine," Carter said.

"Really?" Janice said. Her features twisted, became wry and apologetic, the first genuine expression since she'd entered the bar.

"Of course. We're all grown-ups here." He touched a hand to his chest. "Well, pretty much."

She had the good grace to laugh at that. "I don't know what it is. You're nice, we had a good time..."

"Two and bit dates? No explanation necessary."

"Well, okay." She stood and he did also. "You know, I was considering just not turning up. But you seem like a good guy, I thought I owed you this."

"You don't owe me anything. But I appreciate it. I'll walk you home if you like."

"There's no need. Thanks, though."

They hugged briefly. Janice's waist felt warm beneath her thin dress and Carter felt a stab of regret. Then she turned and left and the regret left with her, replaced by a pang of self-pity that wasn't entirely unpleasant.

He went to the bar and ordered another Peroni. "Apparently I'm a good guy," he said to the barman. The smile he got in return was, Carter thought, understandably wary.

He drank his beer and walked home.

The next morning he woke before six, which he found annoying. It was soon clear that sleep had done with him for the night so he dressed in shorts and a sweat top, washed his face, and did a couple of cursory stretches. He ran occasionally. He didn't enjoy it much but he supposed it was good for him. He found it best to spring such exertion on his body early, before it had time to adjust and complain.

The morning was cool and clear. He lived in a two-story, one bedroom house, part of a recent development next to the river, a two minute walk from the bar he had visited the previous evening.

He stood at his front door and blinked. There was a small passageway between his property and the adjoining house. There was a wheelbarrow in the passageway's entrance, the handles pointing out. He walked around to it. There was a woman laid in the barrow, fully dressed, head thrown back, feet splayed across the handles.

It was Janice and she was dead.

"Try and see this from our point of view, Mr Carter," DI Minto said.

"It's just Carter. How many times?"

DS Walsh said, "Does that matter? Really?"

"Does to me," Carter said.

They were at the Police Station on Bethel Street, in Interview Room 3. It had bare beige walls, a bolted down table and four stark, utilitarian chairs. Carter was comfortable enough, but he was becoming impatient.

Walsh was rail thin, constantly fidgeting. He extracted a Twix bar from his jacket pocket and folded one of the biscuits into his mouth. The other followed moments later. Minto watched him without expression. He was more thickset than his partner, calmer, older too, late thirties, early forties, Carter figured, about the same age as him.

"Did you need that, Gordon?" Minto said. Walsh shrugged, wiping chocolate from the corner of his mouth. Turning back to Carter, Minto said, "I'm just jealous. I've been gaining and losing the same five pounds since Christmas."

Carter patted his own flat stomach. "I hear you."

Minto smiled. It was a good smile. He had a kind face. People would trust him on the basis of that, Carter thought. Most people. "Look, we're not holding you, you're not charged with anything. We'd just like you to go through it one more time."

"I've told you twice." He had, once at the scene with a WPC and again an hour ago, in a different room with Walsh and another constable. Now they'd wheeled

Minto in, like a kindly uncle. Carter had also agreed to a DNA test. Which was fine; for once he had nothing to hide.

"You were the last person to see her alive," Walsh said.

"I clearly wasn't," Carter said.

"That we know of," Minto said quickly, shooting Walsh a warning look.

Walsh shouldered off his jacket and laid it over the back of the chair next to Minto. He had on a short-sleeved lime green shirt, open at the neck. The scruffily knotted navy tie didn't match the shirt. "You don't seem very upset, Mr Carter," he said. "A civilian finding a body, we'd expect more of a reaction."

"I can break down, if you like," Carter said. "If that'll help."

"And someone close," Walsh continued. "Quite a shock."

"We weren't close."

Minto shuffled some papers together, looked up and said, "Three dates?"

"Two and a bit. We weren't close. She seemed like a nice person and I'm sorry for what's happened to her. But no amount of wailing on my part will change anything. Her mother's alive, she has a sister, I think. This is their grief, not mine."

The two policemen were quiet for a moment then Walsh said, "She dumped you, yeah?"

"It was mutual. As I've said."

"How mutual?" Walsh said.

Carter thought for a moment. "To be honest, it was mostly her. But she was right. We were done. It just took me a while to catch on, is all."

"How do you handle rejection?" Minto said, his eyes on his notes.

"Pretty well. Lots of practice."

Minto smiled. Wash said, "So, three dates." He held up a hand, acknowledging Carter's expression. "Two and a bit dates. How far did you get? We're all men of the world here. No need to be shy."

"That's none of your business."

"I mean, we all know what nurses are like, right?" Walsh was leaning against the table now, next to Minto, who laid a hand on his arm.

"Gordon's tone may be a little off, Mr Carter," Minto said, "but I'm afraid it really is our business, all things considered."

Carter waited a moment. "We kissed once, after our second date." He remembered Janice's kiss. It tasted of garlic, but in a good way. Her breath was warm against his throat as he held her, his hands on her slender waist. "That okay with you guys?"

"That was after the pizza at *Brick*," Minto said, consulting his notes again.

"Fast mover," Walsh said, his expression blank.

"We don't all have your charm," Carter said. Minto suppressed a smirk. "Are we done?"

"Almost," Minto looked at him. "You haven't said anything about work."

"What?"

"This is a normal working day for most people. You haven't asked to call the office, anything like that?"

"I'm self-employed."

"Really? Our records are very … sketchy."

"Import, export."

Walsh grunted. "We'll check."

"Knock yourselves out. Now, can I go, or do I need to call someone?"

Minto stood, extending his hand. Carter shook it. "We'll be in touch."

"Don't leave the country," Walsh said.

Funny you should say that, Carter thought.

Eve's place was a twenty minute jog away, a large, plain door in the face of an anonymous block of a building set back in a side street off St Benedicts. Carter pressed the buzzer and said his name. The door opened onto a small ante-chamber containing a desk and a pot plant and a couple of plastic chairs against one wall. A small, elderly white-haired man sat behind the desk.

"Harry," Carter said. Harry nodded. "Is Eve here?"

"I suppose you know the way by now."

"I suppose I do," Carter said.

There was a solid oak door opposite the desk and Carter went through it into a long, wide corridor, with white-painted, windowless doors staggered along each side. At its end the corridor opened up into a wide chamber with three more doors lined up on a long, plain wall. Carter knocked on the middle one and entered.

This room was larger than the chamber Carter had just left. It was an odd combination of treatment room and boudoir, with an adjustable bed and a computer laden desk at one end and an elaborate chaise lounge with matching armchairs and a dark oak dining table at the other. There was an ample, well stocked kitchen attached, Carter knew, along with a bedroom, bathroom and shower.

"Not scheduled, Carter," Eve said. "Not cool."

She was leant against the treatment table, a tall, lean woman with hair as white as Harry's that fell to her waist. Everything about her, apart from the hair, was pared down and economical; the flesh on her hands and face, the way she moved from the table to the desk to check something on the computer.

Carter said, "I can't go to Greece." He told her about Janice and his visit to Bethel Street.

"Fuck's sake," Eve said.

"Can't be helped."

"Who interviewed you? At Bethel Street?"

"Minto and Walsh."

She snorted. "The old good cop, cunt cop routine."

"You know them?"

"I know *of* them. Walsh, at least. Minto, not so much."

"Walsh is all hot air. Anyway, they've got nothing. They can't have."

"I know. Weird, though."

"You're telling me."

"Poor Janice. Do you have any ideas?"

"I don't think it's anything to do with … what we do, if that's what you're worried about."

"I can't deny it crossed my mind. But give me some credit. We go back a long way."

"I'm going all gooey inside."

Eve moved closer to him and sniffed. "Actually, you stink."

"I could do with a shower and a change of clothes."

Eve ushered him towards the bathroom. "You know the way," she said.

He showered and dressed in jeans and a grey, short-sleeved shirt. Eve was in the kitchenette. She handed Carter a tuna sandwich.

"You look hungry," she said.

"Very nurturing. Almost maternal."

"Fuck you."

"Sorry. Thank you is what I meant to say."

"Okay," Eve said, mollified. "Look, do you need a massage? It's what I do, after all. No happy endings, though. I'm too old for all that shit."

"You're the same age as me."

"My point exactly. Amber's free, if that's what you need."

"I'm good, thanks. Sorry about Greece."

"I'll sort it. Don't spend the money. We'll offset it. But I'll be in touch; I might have something else for you. Unless you want to lie low for a bit?"

"It's best to keep busy. Something local would be good, though."

"Not *too* local."

"Well, no. And I'll need the keys to Lawson Road. The house on Riverside is cordoned off."

"No problem." Eve fetched them.

When Carter finished eating, Eve said, "Where to now?"

"I'd better see Jade."

"Jade. You don't think…?"

"Who knows, Eve. She's capable. Probably."

"Jesus. Good luck. You've had your rabies shots?"

Carter almost laughed.

Minto stood by the sink in the kitchen area at Bethel Street. His mug was buried under many other dirty mugs and some bowls and plates.

"I won't bother with a coffee then."

"You're too fussy," Walsh said, pulling an unwashed mug from the pile, rinsing it briefly then filling it with stewed black coffee from a Pyrex pot. Someone had left some Rich Tea biscuits by the fridge and Walsh grabbed a handful and started eating them two at a time.

"Are they yours?" Minto said.

"They are now," Walsh said, through a spray of crumbs. He drank some coffee. "Disgusting," he said. He ate another biscuit.

Minto filled a plastic cup with cold water and took a sip. "I don't think he killed her."

"I don't like him."

"You don't like anyone."

Walsh grunted. "Something's off with him, though."

"Can't argue with that. We'll know more when forensics come back. In the meantime you may as well have a little dig."

"Nothing better to do," Walsh said. He drained his coffee and tossed the mug into the sink, snapping a cereal bowl neatly in two.

Carter walked to Jade's. There were cars he could use if necessary, but he walked if he could and Norwich was small enough that he walked most of the time.

Jade lived in an ex-council house on Victoria Street. Carter had lived there once as well, although that seemed several lifetimes ago.

She answered the door in her dressing gown although it was not yet six o'clock. "What the fuck do you want?" she said. "Have you brought my money?"

"Good to see you too." She was a skinny woman of roughly Carter's height, with unkempt hair and small, bitter eyes. Behind her the living room was explosion of children's clothes and toys and empty spirit bottles. A child, probably a boy, sat on lumpy sofa and stared at him, mouth open, eyes vacant. Carter was fairly sure that he wasn't his. "I need to know what you've been up to, Jade."

He pushed past her into the scruffy room. It smelled faintly of strawberry with an acrylic, chemical undertone. Jade was sucking on rectangular, metallic vaporiser and the fumes released stank of spoiled fruit and solvent. Another mystery solved, Carter thought. He told Jade about Janice.

"What?" Jade said, taking another furious huff on the vaporiser. The smoke engulfed the child, who seemed to neither notice nor care. "You think I did it? You vain bastard. Do you think I give a single solitary fuck where you're sticking your dick these days?" Her head jutted towards Carter as she spoke. He kept his distance as best he could in the crowded room.

"I didn't actually …"

"Again … I … don't … give … a … shit. Just to be clear, I didn't off the bitch. Too busy looking after little lord Fauntleroy here."

Jesus, Carter thought, asking himself yet again what he had ever seen in the withered, bitter woman in front of him. Different times, he told himself. She had changed. A lot. So had he. "Just thought I'd check," he said. "No need to take it so personally."

"No need …" Jade took a long, smoky breath as she gathered herself. "Whatever. Where's my money."

"It's not due till next week."

"You're here now."

"I told you you'd have it, you'll have it."

"Yeah, you once told me you'd love me forever. How's that working out?"

Minto and Walsh were in an unmarked car in the city centre. It was a clear, hot day and they had just been to a council house on the Heartsease Estate to take a statement regarding a minor drugs dispute. Now they were parked on St Benedicts, opposite the Cash Converters.

A dark-haired woman in shorts and a halter top walked past the front of the car. "There are some fine sights on the street today," Walsh said.

"Forgotten you're married again, Gordon?" Minto said.

"I've still got eyes." Minto said nothing. Walsh adjusted his sunglasses as he followed the girl's steps until she was out sight. "You remember, Burns? What he used to say on days like this?" Minto waited. "It's fanny rich out there. That's what Burns used to say."

"Yeah, Burns," Minto said. "He had to resign, didn't he? Suspected sexual misconduct. Lucky not to go down for it, as I recall. Not a great role model, Gordon."

"You're such a prude," Walsh said. He took a chocolate bar from the glove compartment, a Wispa Gold, and unwrapped it. He bit it in half then guided the rest of the bar into his mouth while he was still chewing the first.

Minto looked away. The engine ticked as they waited.

On the Sunday evening after Janice died Carter sat at one of the wooden tables outside the *Adam and Eve*. The warm, dry spell continued and the other tables were full of young, enthusiastic drinkers, all t-shirts and shorts and sunglasses, with tattoos splayed along arms and legs and various parts of exposed torsos. Carter felt old. He had a half pint of Nelson's Revenge left in the glass in front of him. He decided that if the glass was empty and George still hadn't shown up, he'd call it a night and try again in a fortnight.

As if on cue a shambolic scarecrow of a man appeared from the direction of the city centre. He was dressed in blue jeans that were too big at the waist and a rust-coloured sweater over a check shirt. He was carrying a Tesco shopping bag, as he always did. He sat heavily opposite Carter.

"Hell of a day," George said. A young couple opposite turned to stare but then caught the expression on Carter's face and looked away again.

"I didn't think you were coming. Again. I was starting to worry."

George's brow ridged in a confused frown. "I am within our agreed tolerance, am I not?"

"I suppose. It's almost nine."

"Almost."

"It's been three weeks, George. That's odd, is all."

"I've been busy. The computers at the library are inadequate for my purposes. Needs must, I suppose." George was in his forties but he had the bland, smooth features of a teenager. He wore large spectacles that magnified soft, pale eyes that rarely seemed entirely in focus. He ran a hand through a mop of fair hair. "And it closes so often. It's closed now, can you believe that?"

"It's Sunday evening."

George nodded solemnly and looked down at his bony hands as they lay on the wooden table. "Can I have a drink, please?"

Carter fetched two more pints and watched as George took a long draught. "Do you need some food?"

"Food?" George said, as though puzzled by the concept. "No. Of course not. Well, maybe some peanuts." Carter stood to return to the bar. "Dry roasted," George called to his back.

Carter got him two packets and another pint and waited patiently whilst the other man ate the nuts, slowly and methodically, every other mouthful washed down with a tiny sip of beer. The trick with George was to give him time to settle, to feel comfortable in his environment. Or whatever passed for comfortable in George's world.

Twenty years earlier George had been on the verge of completing his mathematics doctorate at the UEA when he suffered a breakdown. He'd attacked two other students during a routine lecture then lapsed into a state of catatonia from which he barely surfaced for over eighteen months. He was sectioned and treated for a variety of mental illnesses then released into sheltered accommodation under medical supervision. He absconded from his flat so many times that the authorities finally gave up and now he lived in various squats around the city, sometimes washing up at a homeless shelter for a few days, for food and a shower.

Carter had known George for a dozen years or so, having intervened in an altercation outside a fish and chip shop in the city centre. A couple of younger men were giving George a hard time but he wouldn't back down. Carter stepped in, guiding George into a nearby pub, where he sipped the pint that Carter had bought for him and said, "I was just trying to explain. They wouldn't listen."

"There's a lot of that about," Carter said. "You can try me, if you like. I'll listen."

George's gaze was soft and unblinking. "Why?"

That's a good question, Carter thought. "Why not?"

George nodded as though that were a satisfactory explanation. "The thing is, I can explain *everything*."

He placed a peculiar emphasis on the last word. Carter didn't realise at the time but George was being entirely literal.

Walsh sat next to Minto at the older policeman's desk. Minto was not entirely happy with the other man's proximity but he tried not to let it show.

Minto had a file open on his computer and they were both peering at it. "Well, that was worth the wait," Walsh said.

Janice Clark had been rendered unconscious by a blow to the back of the head and then suffocated. There was no sign of sexual assault or of any post-mortem interference. The smallest of mercies, Minto thought.

There were no traces of DNA present other than Ms Clark's. There were no fingerprints on the wheelbarrow or any sign of the implement used in the attack, although the assumption was that the barrow and the weapon had been taken from a nearby building site. Confirmation was awaited.

"Anything from the house to house?" Minto said. Walsh shook his head. "Do it again."

"Seriously?"

"I wasn't asking, Gordon."

Walsh sighed heavily and wheeled his chair back to his own desk.

"Anything on Carter?"

"Bugger all," Walsh said. "He doesn't pay any tax and he doesn't claim any benefits. He barely exists, officially. Which these days…"

"None of which makes him a murderer."

"I'd like to get at his bank records, though. I don't suppose we have enough for a warrant?"

"We don't have anything, Gordon," Minto said.

*

"How's it going?" Carter said, when George had finally finished eating.

George glanced at the Tesco bag by his side. It contained, Carter knew, many lined exercise books, all crammed full of equations and calculations written in George's tiny, almost illegible handwriting. "I keep thinking I'm almost there, but then I'm not."

George believed that all of human existence, all that had been and all that was to come, could be captured and explained in a single mathematical equation. After their first couple of meetings Carter had done a little cursory research and found that this was not a unique viewpoint. He mentioned this gently the next time they met, quoting some names he'd gleaned from the internet, clumsily attempting to summarise the current perceived wisdom. George had stared at him for a long moment. "I know of these people. They are simpletons."

"Really, George?"

"SIMPLETONS!" George shouted, his face suddenly crimson, his eyes bulging. Then he stood and left. Carter had been astonished by the outburst, having considered the other man odd but gentle. They had previously agreed, wordlessly it seemed to Carter, to meet every other Sunday at the *Adam and Eve*. If one or other of them hadn't appeared by nine then they the other would call it a day and try again in a fortnight's time. After George's outburst Carter assumed that their meetings were at an end but he waited for the older man dutifully at the appointed time for three consecutive Sundays. On the fourth George was already there, standing by the pub's entrance, bag in hand.

"I would like a pint of lager and some cheese and onion crisps, please," he said, without making eye contact. They drank outside, even though it was November and growing cold. Carter didn't mention any other mathematicians and George didn't turn red and stomp off, so that was good.

"I suppose that's the nature of existence," Carter said.

"Well. No. It really isn't." George's expression and the tone of his voice were deeply patronising, but Carter didn't mind.

"Okay," he said, his own voice heavy with condescension, "You keep trying, I'm sure you'll get there."

George nodded and took another tiny sip of beer. A bee, drugged and lazy, settled on the back of his hand. He watched it for a moment and it flew off.

Carter told George about Janice. "It was inevitable," George said. "I did some calculations." Carter bit his tongue at that. He remembered the other man's blunt indifference when he had told him about his first date with the nurse when they had last met. "Anyway, I have something for you. An offering."

He pulled a crumpled piece of lined paper from a pocket and handed it to Carter. He could just about read George's pencilled scrawl:

"YARMOUTH 3.40 PEACE PROCESS."

"It runs tomorrow," George said.

"What are the odds?"

"Should be about 7-2, something like that."

"Thanks," Carter said. "Another drink?"

The next day Carter took the 13.52 train to Great Yarmouth. He'd spent the morning visiting a number of bookmakers in the city and placing fifty pounds on Peace Process to win in each. George's other obsession, other than the nature of existence, was horse racing. Three or four times a year he would give Carter the name of a horse that, according to his calculations, was certain to win. As it turned out there are no certainties in horse racing, even for George, but his strike rate was in excess of 80%, extraordinarily high and, Carter knew, much better than anything achieved by professional gamblers or tipsters.

Carter, who generally had no interested in racing or gambling, viewed George's tips as an occasional and enjoyable boost to his income. He made sure that he gave George a share of his profits, although the older man had resisted at first. George himself never gambled, although he was always mortified when one of his selections failed to win. On these occasions Carter would attempt to mollify him, explaining that perhaps the going had changed or the horse had messed up the start or gone lame. Either way, it was a profitable aspect of their relationship, although Carter told himself that it was not the only reason that he kept in touch with the man.

He arrived at Yarmouth racecourse in time for the race prior to the 3.40. He took a seat in the grandstand opposite the finishing line and watched the contest without interest. The favourite won, which seemed to please most of the people in Carter's vicinity and there was a muted cry as the winner flashed past, well clear of the rest of the field. Carter wandered over to an ice cream van and bought a 99. As he leant against a retaining wall, eating the ice cream whilst he waited for the odds to appear for the next race, a man in his fifties with a weathered, stubbled face tried to start a conversation. Carter nodded and grunted.

"What do you fancy in the next?"

"I don't gamble," Carter said.

"What are you doing here then?"

"Just passing the time," Carter said, dropping what was left of his cone into a waste basket and wiping his fingers.

The man seemed to consider pushing that further but decided against it and wandered off.

Carter spread a thousand pounds worth of bets amongst the on course bookies, taking a mix of 4's and 3's. Peace Process had shortened to 5-2 by the time the race started.

It was a five furlong sprint, over in a flash. Carter felt no particular excitement as Peace Process took up the running against the stand rail inside the final furlong, pulling readily clear. He wouldn't have felt much if she had lost either. When he was collecting his winnings he found himself next to the man who had tried to talk to him earlier. Carter smiled. The guy gave him a dark look but said nothing.

He treated himself to fish and chips on the seafront before catching the train back to Norwich. He spent an enjoyable couple of hours collecting the rest of his winnings then made his way back to the flat on Lawson Road. When he opened the door there was a large brown envelope waiting for him. There was no writing on the envelope, but Carter knew it was from Eve.

Janice Clark's mother lived alone in a terraced house on the Queen's Hill estate. She was in her seventies, but didn't look it. She was tall and good looking with a bearing that Minto more readily associated with the owner of a country home. Not that there was anything wrong with Mrs Clark's house, which was scrupulously clean and neat, if devoid of any particular character. But Minto knew that drugs were dealt in the nearby alleys and the underpass across the way. For no particular reason, he felt that this woman deserved better.

He sat in an armchair; Mrs Clark was bolt upright on the sofa opposite. Next to her was her surviving daughter, Natalie, Janice's older sister. Minto had seen photographs of the dead woman, of course – indeed there were several on display atop the sideboard to his right – and the similarity was unmistakeable. Natalie was perhaps a little taller, more her mother's stature, but her features were that of her sister, pretty and understated.

Minto was alone, Walsh having called in sick the last couple of days. He found that he was not sorry. There was a pot of coffee on the table between them along with an impressive array of biscuits. Minto imagined Walsh setting waste to them and, amid the carnage, hitting on the bereaved sister, if not the mother. Anyway, Minto enjoyed working alone.

Mrs Clark had asked a question that most, if not all, relatives of a murder victim ask and Minto was considering his answer. "I am as certain as I can be that your daughter didn't suffer," Minto said. "She was knocked unconscious, from behind, without warning. There is no sign of any…" His voice faltered. He had been determined to remain professional and direct but he was finding the older woman's unblinking gaze hard to take.

"Thank you, Detective Inspector," Mrs Carter said. "That is some … comfort."

"John, please."

She looked at him again, without speaking. Her eyes were clear and dry. The room was hot, stifling even. Natalie had her hand on her mother's shoulder, rubbing it gently through a thin cotton cardigan.

"How is it going?" Natalie said. She spoke more quickly than her mother. There was some Norfolk in her voice but not very much. "The investigation. If you are at liberty to say, of course."

Minto sipped his tea and placed the cup carefully onto the table, stalling. There was nothing *to* say. The wheelbarrow had been taken from the nearby building site as suspected, but there was no sign of whatever had been used to knock Janice unconscious. The best guess was a spanner or crowbar but the contractor responsible for the building site confirmed that only the barrow was missing. There were two CCTV cameras in the vicinity but neither was working during the night in question. Further door to door enquiries had turned up nothing at all, which, in Minto's experience was unheard of. Carter remained of interest but there was absolutely no physical evidence to link him to the crime. "I am so sorry, Ms Clark ... my hands are tied. I promise you will be the first to know when ..." He hesitated again.

"I understand. And if you're John, then I'm Natalie." A smile, brief and cold, but something. More than I deserve, Minto thought.

Natalie took her hand from her mother's shoulder. The older woman gazed absently at the spot where it had been. Earlier Minto and Natalie had worked their way through the contacts on Janice's mobile phone, eliminating them of suspicion. It had seemed odd to Minto that Carter's details had not been on the phone, but the older sister had shrugged that off. "It never amounted to much."

Now, as Natalie showed him to the door, he said, "Is there anything else you can tell me about your sister's relationship with Mr Carter?"

"Relationship? A couple of dates?"

Two and a bit, Minto thought. "I take your point. Still ... anything?"

"She didn't mention him much. He was a nice guy, though. She liked him."

"She still dumped him."

"Well, yes. I doubt that had anything to do with him."

"I'm sorry?"

Natalie hesitated. Her mother had gone upstairs and Natalie made sure that she was out of earshot. It was warm in the hallway but her shoulders were hunched, her arms drawn across her chest, her hands tucked into the sleeves of her blouse. Her voice was hushed. "Jan had a fiancé, a couple of years ago. It ended ... badly. She never really got over it."

Minto pulled his notebook from a jacket pocket. "I'm surprised that you haven't mentioned this before, Ms Clark. Do you have a name? The fiancé? I'll need to talk to him."

"The thing is, he's dead."

"What?"

"He killed himself after Janice finished with him."

In the envelope that Eve had left him were, amongst other things, the keys to a steel grey hatchback so nondescript that Carter hardly noticed it parked on the roadside very early on the Wednesday after he had met George.

When he did find it he dumped a canvas bag full of essentials onto the passenger seat then drove, without a break, the 235 miles to a small village on the outskirts of York. He passed through the village once then pulled into a thick wooded area a couple of miles on. Ensuring he was not visible from the road he took the envelope from the glove compartment and reviewed the contents again. There were a number of photographs of a thickset man in his fifties with grey hair cut short at the sides and thinning on top, along with enough information about his life and usual movements that Carter could have written a biography if he so wished. Also there were details of the village, CCTV blind spots, policing and other miscellanea.

When he'd seen enough he took a bottle of water, a banana and a protein bar from the bag and ate and drank slowly. Then he waited.

When it was dark Carter walked into the village. He wore dark jeans and a black, hooded, zip-through sweatshirt. There was a pub on the village's main street with flower baskets hanging by the door and a number of wooden seats abutting the pavement. Further on, past the post office and a church, there was a wide turning to the left that led to the Conservative Club and row of pretty, detached houses. The club backed onto a large wooded area. Carter took a circuitous route and waited in the woods with a view of the rear of the club, chiefly of a door that led to the bar and kitchen. He knew that the man in the photos worked at the club from time to time and tended the bar on Wednesday evenings. He was a smoker and he took regular breaks. The club was quiet most Wednesdays.

Now Carter watched as the grey-haired man slipped out through the rear door and lit a cigarette. He smoked with some relish, fumes pluming through his nostrils in thin, grey jets. He consulted his phone briefly, as people do, swiping idly through a number of screens. After eight minutes he flicked the cigarette stub away and slipped back inside.

Carter snapped on a pair of thin rubber gloves and waited some more.

Fifty-three minutes later the man stepped through the plain white door once again. He had a cigarette in his mouth but he didn't light it immediately, seemingly having found something of interest on his phone. Carter was already moving towards him with brisk, silent purpose and he was in the other man's shadow before he was noticed. The older man's head jerked up and his eyes widened. He didn't speak and the unlit cigarette remained clamped between his lips. Carter pulled a small sharp knife from the pocket of his sweatshirt and ran the blade across the other man's throat in a single, smooth motion. He was already moving away with the last sweep of the knife, clear of the arterial spray. He kept walking and didn't look back.

A couple of days later Minto and Walsh were parked in a layby in their unmarked car. Walsh was hunched over a Tupperware container, picking at the salad within. It was his first day back at work after sick leave. He looked pale and thinner than ever, Minto thought.

"There was no need to rush back, Gordon."

Walsh dropped a black plastic fork into the salad and snapped the container lid shut. "I look like shit, is what you're trying say."

"Honestly? You've looked better."

"I've got to work, John. I was crawling up the walls. You know what I mean." Minto did. "Look, they're running some tests. I should hear back next week."

"What sort of tests?"

"Blood tests, urine tests. Any other bodily fluids they can think of. In the meantime I'm meant to address my lifestyle."

"Really?"

"Hence the rabbit food. But what the fuck do they know?"

"What indeed."

Walsh ignored the sarcasm. "So, the nurse's ex? Anything useful there?"

"He's dead, Gordon."

"Yeah, yeah. He must have some family. Someone who bears a grudge, perhaps? Be nice to find a trace of a motive."

"The father's dead, mother's in a home. There is an older brother. Dan's looking into him. You can lend a hand if you want. Make yourself useful."

Walsh grunted his assent. "One good thing. Did you hear about that pedo up north? Another piece of scum taken off the board."

"He was cleared."

"On a technicality, John. Everyone knows he was guilty. And he would have done it again."

"That's the third one in six months. Sounds like some sort of vigilante. We can't condone that kind of thing."

"Yeah, we don't have to cry about it either. Or break our necks catching the guy."

"Jesus," Minto said.

It was early the next Sunday morning and Carter wasn't expecting a visitor. He peered through the peephole, then pulled his head back for a moment, considering. Then he looked again before opening the door.

"Good job I don't believe in ghosts," he said.

"I don't look that much like her," Natalie Clark said. "Can I come in?"

Carter opened the door wider and beckoned her through. "How did you find me?"

"John Minto."

Carter nodded as though that made sense. Natalie brushed past him. He recognised her scent. It was the same one that Janice had worn for their first two dates.

"Spartan," she said, standing in the doorway to the living room. She had a point. Bare white walls and ceiling; a couple of beige rugs thrown across a pine wood floor; a functional sofa with two matching chairs; a large flat screen TV affixed to the wall opposite the sofa.

"I am a man of simple needs."

Natalie smiled. She had on a plain summer dress with strappy high heeled shoes. She wore make up as though *this* was a date. She had her hair the same way that Janice had the last time he had seen her alive. "Can I smoke?" she said, her hand already snaking into her tan leather bag.

"No."

If Natalie was affronted she didn't show it. "I can sit though?"

"Be my guest."

She sat primly on one of the chairs, legs pressed together, leant forward, hands palm down on her bare knees.

"What do you want?"

"Tea? Coffee? Anything's fine."

"That's not what I meant," Carter said.

"Oh." Natalie's gaze slid downwards although the smile remained in place. Then her face came up again and tilted towards Carter who was stood in the doorway, arms folded. "Curious, I suppose."

"Curious?"

"Yes. Look, please come and sit down. I won't keep you, I promise."

Carter took the chair opposite. "I am sorry about your sister," he said.

Natalie nodded. "To be honest," she said, "I'm not."

"Okay."

"I didn't like her, Mr Carter."

"It's just Carter."

"In fact, I hated her. Always have. I was pleased when I heard. Pleased." She put a hand flat on her chest. Her nails were painted burgundy. "I felt a thrill, right here. What does that say about me?"

"There's law no against it."

"She was a bitch."

"She seemed perfectly..."

"She was a fucking bitch, Carter. I knew her, you didn't. She had everyone fooled. Mum ... well, she was always mum's favourite, from the moment she popped out. It was all about Janice."

"Did you tell Minto any of this?"

"No. Of course not. I told him about Brian, though."

"Brian?"

"She didn't mention Brian? Of course she didn't." Her hands were clenched in front of her, her knuckles taut and white. "Her fiancée. He was lovely. I liked, Brian. I liked him very much."

"What happened?"

"She dicked him around. Kept setting dates for the wedding, then cancelling. She accused him of ... all sorts of things. She was jealous and petty and ... in the end he couldn't take it anymore. She dumped him for the last time and he went and hanged himself."

"I'm sorry."

"Sorry," she said, without looking at him. "Yeah, we were all sorry. Except Janice, of course."

"So, this Brian, did he have any ..."

"Minto's been through all that. He had a brother, he's looking into it, for what it's worth. It won't be him. He was fucking useless. Not a patch on Brian." Her eyes came up to his. They were dry and empty. "They think you killed her."

"I didn't."

"I don't give a shit if you did. Did you fuck her, Carter?"

"I don't ..."

"Most everyone did. You can fuck me if, if you like. Now. On the sofa. I don't mind."

"Jesus," Carter said.

"Or not. Look, can I smoke?"

"You need to leave."

She looked at her watch and stood suddenly. "I'm late. I said I'd take mum to church. Can you believe that?"

He ushered her to the door. On the pavement she turned and waved. Her smile was grotesque. Back inside the scent of her perfume lingered.

Later he called Minto and they met at a wooden bench next to the duck pond in Waterloo Park.

"How did you know where to send the sister?" Carter said. They stood by the bench, facing each other. The day was clear and still.

"I followed you." Carter nodded. "What did she have to say? Natalie?"

Carter considered telling the truth, but only briefly. "Nothing much. Just curious."

"Curious?"

"Women. What can I say?"

"Don't give me that, Carter."

"I don't know. Closure, perhaps?"

"Did she mention the fiancé?"

"Brian? A little. Anything there?"

"A brother. He's got an alibi. So has Natalie. So has everyone. Except you, Carter."

"Funny."

"I'm not joking."

"Come on."

Minto's shoulders slumped. He brushed the bench clean and sat, legs crossed, gazing at the pond. A duck eyed him warily. "Should have bought some bread."

"It's not good for them. Apparently."

"Bloody hell. Is nothing sacred?"

Carter sat next to the detective. "Where's Walsh?"

"Hospital. Intensive care. Heart attack."

Carter almost said that he was sorry, but he didn't want to add hypocrisy to his already long list of sins. "They didn't get you another partner?"

"Cuts. That's how we roll these days."

"Time was, a murder in Norwich, you'd throw everything at it."

"Resources, Carter. It's not high profile. She's from a council house background. There's no money there. No sexual angle." He aimed an imaginary gun at the duck. It turned away and slid into the still water. "Post-Brexit Britain. Nobody gives a shit about anything anymore."

"I didn't have you down as a cynic, Minto."

"What else would I be?" Minto shifted in his seat and extracted a notebook from a jacket pocket. "There is one thing. We got a call back from a guy lives near you. He left to go on holiday early on the morning that Janice died and he's only just back." He peered at the open book. "He saw someone, just as he was leaving. Tall guy, forties. Skinny and scruffy with wild hair. Mean anything to you?"

"Not a thing. Sorry, Minto."

"It was a long shot." He tucked the book back into the pocket. "It's something though."

Carter stood. "Good luck. Hope Walsh pulls through."

"Walsh," Minto said, as though he had forgotten about him. "Yeah. Sure."

Minto left. Carter stood by the pond trying to fit his thoughts in place when two things happened, one after the other.

First Jade called.

"Someone's following us. Creepy dude. Is this anything to do with you, Carter?"

"Describe him." Jade did. "Where are you?"

"At home."

"Is he there now?"

"No, but he was outside last night and he was at the park yesterday when Jake was playing on the swings."

There was a beep on the line, indicating another incoming call. Ignoring it, Carter read out an address. "Go there, take the boy. Say that I sent you."

"Why? Who is this …"

"Just do it, Jade."

There was a moment's silence, then, "Where's my fucking money, Carter."

He hung up. There was a message from Eve. Carter listened to it.

"Carter. Jesus. There's someone here. Harry … Jesus. Just get here, Carter. Now."

The door was slightly ajar and Carter pushed through it, breathing heavily. The desk was on its side in the middle of the ante-chamber, the two plastic chairs were on their backs at opposite ends of the small room. Harry was curled in a foetal position next to the desk. His hands were linked above his head but the fingers were smashed and broken as was the top of his skull. Eve was knelt next to him, a hand on his arm. She wore a white blouse. It was dotted with blood but Carter didn't think it was hers.

"He's dead," Eve said without looking up.

"The other girls?"

"Locked in their rooms. Like I was until a minute ago. Harry buzzed through, warning me."

"How did he get in?"

"Gave your name, Harry said. Then there was a grunt and I heard the blows. I heard him die, Carter."

"Anything else?"

"He hammered on some doors, yelled a bit. I saw him through the peephole. Tall guy. Thin. Looked like he was homeless. He …"

"I know who he is, Eve."

"What?" She looked at him for the first time. Her eyes were wide, her mouth open.

"I'll sort it," Carter said.

George was sitting at one of the wooden tables outside the *Adam and Eve* when Carter found him. The shopping bag was at his feet and he had three blue exercise books open in front of him along with a large piece of graph paper, on which he was writing in pencil. George was hunched over the paper and his tongue protruded slightly from between thin lips. It was early evening and clouds were gathering as the air cooled.

Carter moved into George's eye line and the other man's head came up. "Can I have a drink, please?" George said.

"In a minute," Carter said. "But I think we need to talk. Don't you?"

"Drink first. Then talk." He spoke slowly, like a child. There was a smudge of blood on the front of George's rust-coloured sweater, Carter noticed. There was some on his face as well and in his hair.

Carter relented and fetched two pints. He sat opposite the other man and waited.

"There is no now," George said eventually, staring at his drink. "The moment you consider it, it's gone."

"That does tend to be the nature of things."

"Do you have any idea how hard it is to plot this moment? And this one? And this?"

"No. Of course I don't. But you don't have ..."

"I do," George said. He put his hands face down on the piece of graph paper in front of him. A thin line of drool fell slowly from the side of his mouth. "But I can't." His voice was utterly flat and defeated.

"Why did you kill Janice?"

"She was an offering. To you. Like the horses I give you. She would not have made you happy. I could work that out at least."

"We were finished."

"You told me."

"After you killed her."

"Yes." George sighed. "But in the scheme of things ... a single life ... what does it matter?"

"And Harry?"

"Harry?"

"The old guy at the massage parlour?"

"Massage parlour." George's smile was thin and wintry. "It's a front. They had you killing pederasts."

"How the hell did you know ..."

"I followed you."

"Followed me? You don't even drive ..."

George pulled a handful of the exercise books from the shopping bag and threw them on the table. "I followed you. And I keep up with the news. How long before you're caught? They'll put you away."

"I ..."

"You're my only friend, Carter."

Carter stared at the other man. "Jesus Christ, George."

"I'm going to walk to the car park on St Stephen's now. I'm going to climb to the top and jump off."

"Don't be stupid."

"I should have done it a long time ago."

"We can get you help. I know people."

"The thing with jumping is, go over head first. People make the mistake of leading with their feet. That can be messy and not particularly quick. Don't worry, I won't do that."

"I can't let you do this."

George picked up one of the books and flicked through the pages. "Of course you can. You already have." He reached into his jeans pockets and produced two pieces of paper. "This one has the location of the weapon I used on the girl. And this is another horse. Newmarket, two days time. I hope it wins." He stood.

"At least finish your drink first, George."

"I'm not thirsty any more. I'm not anything."

George walked off and Carter watched him. After a couple of minutes it started to rain, the drops splashing into the untouched glasses of beer. Then it grew heavier and the graph paper and the exercise books soon became sodden, the tiny pencil handwriting smudged and indecipherable.

"Developments," Minto said. They were in Waterloo Park again. The DI stood by the duck pond with his hands in his pockets. "We had a jumper, couple of nights ago. Went off the car park in St Stephens. Homeless guy, matches the description of the man seen the night Janice died."

"Interesting." Carter stood also. The wooden bench was too wet from the recent rain for them to sit. The earth was rich and damp beneath their feet.

"Then we had a call. Anonymous. Led us to a squat on Magdalen Street. We found an iron bar, under what presumably passes for a bed. DNA match to the victim and the guy who jumped."

"That's all very tidy," Carter said.

"It's a result, is what it is. Nobody cares how we got there."

"It fair gladdens the heart," Carter said.

"What?"

"Nothing. How's Walsh?"

"On the mend. Flirting with the nurses. One of them made a complaint."

"Figures. So, do I get an apology now?"

"For what?"

"You thought I was a murderer."

"It was an honest mistake. No apology."

"Fair enough," Carter said.

Later the same day Carter backed the horse that George had given him. It won.

The Way You Look At Me

Two days after the second vote the bomb went off. I felt it rather than heard it, stood in our kitchen, cradling a mug of coffee, staring out of the window at nothing much. The frame shuddered a fraction and a tremor shook the tiled floor and rippled through my bare feet into my shins, my thighs, my groin.

"Sarah," I said, as though she was there.

The car bomb exploded outside a pub on the Earlham Road at 5.13 am on the first Tuesday in June. Many expressed surprise that Norwich had been chosen as the initial target. London was considered the more obvious choice. Or Brighton perhaps. Both cities would take their turn in the weeks to come. The pub was in its own grounds, walled off, set back a little from the road. It was owned and run by a prominent remain supporter but the only person on the premises at the time of the explosion was a cleaner. He was killed instantly.

Sarah meets me later that week, in a café on Ber Street. She arrives first and I see her before she sees me. She looks forlorn, I think. The heatwave has not relented and she's wilting a little, trapped in a slab of hot light. She wears a jacket, though, for some reason, buttoned to the throat, despite the sweat in her blond fringe. The toes of her feet point slightly inwards. My heart breaks a little, although I'm not sure why.

She turns, sensing me. She doesn't stop me kissing her cheek.

"You're late," she says.

"Just barely. Anyway, I've been shopping." I hold up a plastic Sainsbury's bag. "I've got you a present."

She peers inside. "Chocolates."

"Green and Black's."

"You shouldn't have."

"I know you like them."

"No, you really shouldn't. I'm on a diet, Rob. You know I'm on a diet."

"You don't need to be."

"Well, I am." She reaches into the bag. "Anyway, they're melting."

Of course they are, I think, following her into the café.

It's the lull between breakfast and lunch and the place is almost empty. Sarah takes a seat in an alcove and I walk to the counter to order. No food for Sarah, just tea. I ponder the chalkboard above the counter. A feather light, willowy guy in a t-shirt and jeans comes over and looks at me expectantly.

"Tea. Coffee. Bacon bap, no sauce. Chocolate cake."

He nods while he rings the items up on the till. A radio burbles behind him. Some phone in, discussing the bomb. I catch the odd word or two over the hum of the air-conditioning; outrage, Russian money, will of the people. Same old stuff, over and over. I pinch the skin at the bridge of my nose and close my eyes.

"Ten fifty five," the man says, hand outstretched. He has a small mouth, white teeth, tufty outposts of hair on his chin and cheeks.

I take the money. "Can you put something else on?"

"You not interested? This is massive, man."

"Yeah, I know. It's just …"

"I mean, the guy who died? Turns out he was a leaver. Ironic or what?"

"Yeah. Ironic."

I join Sarah, sit opposite her on a too-small wooden chair. She's removed her jacket, revealing a thin, cherry-coloured sweater.

"Making a new friend?" she says.

"You know me."

"Did you ask for some water?"

"No."

She shrugs.

"You look hot," I say.

She raises an eyebrow.

"Not that sort of hot."

The eyebrow shoots up a little further.

"Well, of course, *that* sort of hot as well…"

"You can stop digging, Rob."

The corner of her mouth twists and the flesh around her eyes creases a little. A glimmer of the old Sarah, the old us.

The guy from the counter comes over carrying two glasses of iced water.

"Thought you might need these," he says, looking at Sarah.

She gives him a great smile, full wattage, all eyes and teeth. "Thanks. That's so sweet."

"No problem. Your tea won't be long."

She thanks him again. As she turns back to me the

years clamber back onto her face and she's early forties again, not late-twenties after all.

"So," she says, a hand flicking involuntarily to her eyes, her nose, her mouth.

"I'm still taking the tablets."

"Good."

"Is it? Look at me." I grip my belly where it sags over the waistband of my too-tight jeans. It's not just that; even my facial features have thickened and coarsened. Every part of me feels heavy and alien.

"That's the pills, is it?"

On cue the slender guy brings our drinks and my food. We move some flowers and condiments to one side to make room. Butter drips from the crevasses of the bacon roll. Thick, rich icing glues the vast slab of cake to the plate.

"It's my lunch," I say weakly.

"It's just gone eleven."

"I didn't have any breakfast." It's a lie and Sarah knows it. I sip my coffee. It's too hot and it burns my lips and tongue. "Fuck's sake," I say. Sarah sighs. I look at the coffee cup and then at the condensation beading my water glass.

At the second referendum, by some kind of dark symmetry, the nation voted 52 to 48 to re-join the European Union under exactly the same terms as when they'd left five years earlier. Old wounds were not healed. The acrimony that had grown, fuelled by the mismanagement of successive, tin-eared governments, deepened into something tangible and ripe; a kind of ersatz civil war. It was waged mostly on social media, but also spilled onto the streets as a dozen protesters died in separate civil disturbances in the run up to the second vote. The political parties shape-shifted, attempting to second-guess the demands of a febrile, bovine electorate. They mostly lurched to the extremes, the dark fringes, places unthinkable only a decade earlier. Most of the media followed them, willingly enough.

I eat quickly as always, eyes cast down. When I've finished I say, "I was worried. About you. When the bomb went off."

"I was miles away."

"I didn't know."

"I was at my mother's. Where else would I be?"

"I didn't know," I say again. "I didn't know anything." I want to ask, were you worried? About me? The answer is in her silence and in the set of her mouth but I want to ask her anyway. "How is your mother?"

She gives a half-pout, her slender fingers extending, covering the rim of her tea cup. "How do you think? Hard work, as always."

"Her or me. Talk about a rock or a hard place." There is a third option, of course, although it remains unspoken for now. But I can see it in her eyes when we meet and sense it in the curtness of her text messages. I used to get four kisses once upon a time. Now I don't get any. Now I barely warrant a full sentence.

She sits back suddenly. Her eyes meet mine then skitter away again. "How long is it going to be, Rob? How long are you going to be … like this?" Her voice has become whiny, childish, small. It doesn't suit her. It turns me on a little, though. Go figure.

"Well that's a question. I know it's hard. For you."

"It *is* hard." She doesn't pick up on the lack of inflection in my voice. "This isn't what I expected. You used to be so …"

I wait for her to elaborate but she doesn't. "Thank goodness we didn't marry."

"That's what mum said."

"Is it? Bless her," I say. I stretch out my hand so that it rests next to my glass. My flesh appears to be the same colour as the water. I wonder, briefly, if I am actually there at all.

Later it was as though no-one was entirely sure who was responsible for the second referendum. Government was fluid. Statements were opaque. Truth became an abstraction, something malleable, negotiable even. As democracy calcified small groups gathered in the streets of Stoke, Stevenage, Bolton, Lewisham. Men, mostly, young and old. Families making a day of it. The windows of shops owned by non-whites were smashed, premises burned. Sometimes people died. Few seemed to care.

Business is picking up as lunchtime approaches. The young guy is joined by a girl of similar age and build. They appear weightless, gliding between the tables. The girl has long blond hair and is heartbreakingly pretty. I try to attract her attention to order more coffee but she looks right through me.

Sarah talks about her mother; how she's smoking again, how she does nothing but moan. Sarah talks about how narrow her own life has become. She needs a good night out, she says. She needs something for *her*.

Sarah asks if I'm keeping my appointments. I say that I am. I say that at our last meeting the counsellor said, "You know, Rob, what you really need to do is cut out those negative thoughts."

The incredulity of it is fresh in my mind and I look up at Sarah to see her reaction. Her eyes and mind are elsewhere. "Perhaps he has a point," she says.

"If only I'd thought of it earlier," I say. I'm fairly sure that I can see the grain of the table through the flesh of my right hand. "I'd better be off."

"What will you do with your afternoon?"

I'll stare at a single point on the wall in our living room for four hours straight while the fire in my mind subsides, I think. "Not much," I say. "Same time next week?"

"I suppose," she says, standing.

There's a commotion by the counter. The willowy guy turns the radio up. "There have been more attacks," he announces with a kind of unfocused relish. "Bombs in London, a knife attack in Southampton."

"Jesus," someone says.

We reach the door. I want to get out of there, but Sarah lingers.

"Any fatalities?" someone else says.

"Loads by the sounds of it," the guy says. His eyes are bright. He's enjoying this a little too much.

I push my way out of the door into the stupid, visceral heat. Sarah follows a moment later.

"I mean, I did say that this would happen. A year ago, two years ago. I said …"

"I know, Rob," Sarah snaps. "I know because it was me that you said it to. Over and over. Well done. You were right."

I don't know what to say so I don't say anything. Sarah carries her jacket over her left arm as we walk slowly towards the city centre.

The streets are becoming busy as office workers turn out for lunch. As we approach the end of Ber Street a large black Ford van parks erratically across the road from us, in front of the food importers. Its brakes scream as it stops suddenly and the back doors open and two men dressed in black tumble out. The driver spills out onto the road also. Like the others he wears a balaclava. He is carrying what looks like a machete in his right hand.

I turn to Sarah. Her mouth and eyes are wide open. There's an alley to her left that leads to Surrey Street and the city centre. I push her towards it. "Go," I say, "Get help."

She turns, hair flying. I feel a hand tug at my arm for the briefest moment and then she's gone. It occurs to me that she's left the chocolates I bought her in the café. Which seems a shame.

A siren blares from miles away. The three men gather themselves. They all carry blades of some kind. The scene is covered in a wash of tired light. Colours are muted and drained in the relentless heat. It feels as though I'm looking through a filter. It reminds me of the home videos we had back in the seventies, when I was still alive.

Two of the men peel off and head towards the city centre. The other turns towards me. I am aware suddenly of the sour tang of my own scent. The man's balaclava partially covers his mouth. The thin material is sucked against his lips then expelled again by his rapid, ragged breaths. He appears to be wheezing. Maybe he has asthma. The hand that grasps the machete is pale and covered with fine grey hairs. He moves towards me but very slowly. I think of Zeno's paradoxes. Perhaps he will never reach me at all.

I look up. A pair of contrails intersect in a cloudless sky.

Vinegar Lake

The wind came in hard that night, hunting through the dark streets. It swept in low, close to the ground, slapping saplings flat, snapping fence posts, seeking the soft wood and cuffing it aside.

Jenny slept through it. I didn't try. I stood on the lawn to the rear of our house, in t-shirt and boxer shorts, waiting for it. The first blow drove me back a couple of steps, flattening cotton against chest and thighs, punching the breath from my lungs. I threw my head back. It was moments before I could breathe. I tasted warm air as small pieces of debris pin-wheeled past my face. Falling to my knees I tried to laugh but the wind wouldn't allow it.

The rain came later, as the wind dropped, soaking me instantly. At around dawn the weather lost interest in our particular part of Norfolk. The sky emptied and the morning, when it arrived, was bland and innocent.

It was a Sunday and Jenny had already eaten breakfast by the time I rose. She was in the conservatory watering her pot plants.

"Here he is," she said, without looking up. "The storm chaser."

"You slept well."

"You could at least have wiped your feet before you came in. I don't enjoy cleaning your filthy paw prints off the kitchen floor."

"I'd have done it."

"You know I can't leave it like that." Her voice was mild. Her voice was always mild. I can hardly recall her speaking above a gentle, lulling monotone in over thirty years.

"The plants look well."

She almost looked at me then but instead she gave a soft snort and continued watering. "Name one."

"What? I dunno. Brian?"

"That's very funny, Stephen."

"They're your thing, my darling; as has long since been established."

"My thing," Jenny said, standing up straight, stretching a little, the small green watering can hanging limply from her right hand. "I suppose it is."

I ate breakfast and drank a pot of strong tea while Jenny showered and dressed. My feet were coated with dirt. I smelled of old rain and wet earth. I remembered how the wind felt during the night, the heat of it as it screamed into my open mouth. I remembered wishing that every one of my atoms could be torn apart and reassembled.

I was still in a reverie, arms braced against the kitchen worktop, head bowed, when Jenny entered. Her scent preceded her, something fresh and floral.

"You haven't forgotten, have you? We're hosting tonight. Richard and Chloe. Drinks and nibbles."

"Drinks and nibbles. How could I forget?" She cleared away my breakfast things, working around me, wiping down the worktop. "I think I'll go as I am."

She paused and turned to face me, arms at her side, hands linked in front of her. "And what would Chloe think of that?"

"She might fancy a bit of rough."

Jenny made a noise in the back of her throat and looked towards the kitchen window. Her clothes were soft-edged and elegant. The colours she chose were gentle, muted. Jenny met no resistance as she moved through the world. There were no edges to catch, nothing abrasive or difficult. Except me, perhaps.

"Anyway, church." Her head swept round and she glanced past me at the clock on the wall, at the print next to it; a bottle of red wine, some grapes. "You can come, if you like. There's still time, if you hurry."

"Every week the same," I said.

"I have to ask."

Yes, I thought, apparently you do.

After Jenny left I tidied the garden. Our fence posts were sturdily constructed so most of the debris that I gathered into a rough pile was from neighbouring properties. Not that there was anyone too close by: we were at the edge of the village and wild meadows buffered our boundaries on either side.

We had too much land. Jenny may have been mildly obsessed with indoor plants but her interest did not extend to our garden. We had a couple of acres, mostly rough, undulating lawn, with a few half-hearted flower beds here and there; some fuchsias, some roses, azaleas for later in the summer. I'd started a vegetable patch a couple of years back but it was forlorn and weed-encrusted now. George, an old guy from the village, dropped in a twice a month to prevent things getting too out of hand.

*

"This house," Chloe said, as she swept past Jenny into our hallway, her eyes cast upwards at the high ceiling and the wide, immaculate, cream-coloured walls. She'd said the same thing on the previous occasions that she'd visited in the half year or so since her and Jenny had become friends. They'd met through the church, of course. She cooed her way through the kitchen, fingers trailing across the marble-topped island, then past the Aga and towards the living room.

"Make yourself at home," I said.

"Stephen, darling." She came towards me and kissed my cheek. Her scent was much heavier than Jenny's. "I always do. You know that. You look terrific, by the way."

Did I? I'd made a bit of an effort, I suppose; a fresh new shirt, jeans, a light linen jacket. Chloe was vibrant in a flowered summery dress. She wore her auburn hair short, cut neatly around her ears. She was tallish and slender with pale skin and grey eyes that brimmed with a curious light.

When Jenny came into the room she seemed muted by comparison. Beautiful, but of less substance; not entirely of this dimension. The dress that she wore was a cornflower-blue that matched the walls of the living room. It was as though she was camouflaged. It was sometimes difficult to tell where the house ended and she began.

Richard trailed in behind Jenny. He was a big man, tall and broad. His hair was very dark and obscenely lustrous for someone in their mid-fifties. My hand went involuntarily to the soft, thinning burr of my own scalp.

"Stephen." He loomed towards me, his fist engulfing mine. "How the hell are you?"

His presence overwhelmed me, as did his scent, which was musky and expensive. I felt something tick in my blood as I tried to smile. "Fine. Thanks."

"Good man." He squeezed my hand. His face was too close to mine.

"Put the poor boy down," Chloe said from across the room.

He released his grip, laughing. The early evening sun dipped and refracted light filtered through the large picture window that made up one wall. Primary colours fell across Chloe's face and neck.

We ate outside. Jenny served Negroni with ham and pear crostini and bacon-wrapped dates. Then we had soft roasted peppers and artichoke with warm olive bread and a bone-dry Manzanilla sherry.

I listened mostly. It was mid-June and it was some time before the light softened and the shadows grew bolder, encroaching upon the decking and the bespoke sofa upon which Jenny and Chloe sat. They spoke about church matters; committees that they were on, fundraising issues, the new vicar.

Chloe liked him, Richard didn't.

"He's black," Chloe said.

"Nothing to do with that," Richard said, folding his legs awkwardly. "I just don't like his energy, that's all."

"His energy?" Jenny said.

"He's perfectly charming," Chloe said. "You like him, don't you, Jen?"

"He's fine."

"High praise," I said.

They all looked at me for a moment. I sipped my sherry. To the east, beyond Chloe and Jenny, the sun was setting in peach and cherry-coloured layers, like some indulgent dessert.

As the light died we came inside and drank brandy in the living room. We sat in couples, opposite each other, nobody touching.

Richard talked about work, as he often did. I admired his confidence, his unvoiced assumption that anyone would actually give a shit.

"Thing is, small businesses, we're literally drowning in red tape."

"Literally," I said.

"Don't be tiresome, Stephen." He said it indulgently, with a smile. I didn't mind. "We're a different breed, I suppose; entrepreneurs." He stumbled over the word. The drink was showing in his face as well; his jowls were ruddy and his ample, handsome, nose had become veined and prominent.

"I suppose you are."

He ignored that, although I wondered for a moment if he would. Richard, as he never tired of telling anybody who would listen, was a self-made man. This had mostly entailed, from what I could gather, taking an extremely healthy nest egg, left by his father, and eroding it steadily through a succession of increasingly desperate property deals. I ached to ask him exactly what he would be worth if he had simply invested his father's inheritance in the first place. Perhaps after a couple more brandies I would.

"You wouldn't know," he said, draining his glass. "Not your fault."

"Well, you can't be doing too badly," I said. "Chloe's still around, after all."

I felt Jenny's gaze snap upon the side of my face. "Stephen."

Chloe's smile, across from me, was angled and obtuse.

Richard's laugh was loud and sudden. "Nice one," he said. "Nice one, Stephen. It's a poor excuse of a man who can't laugh at himself. Isn't that right?"

"As I'm sure the good Lord himself would attest," I said, raising my glass and tipping it towards Richard.

He looked understandably puzzled but lifted his glass in response anyway. His puzzlement deepened when he realised that the glass was empty.

Jenny stepped forward to offer a refill. I saw Richard glance down the front of her dress as she leant before him. Chloe noticed too and then our eyes met briefly and she suppressed a smirk as she looked away.

Jenny settled again. "I don't know what's wrong with you this evening, Stephen."

"This evening?" Richard said.

It was my turn to laugh. It was short and bitter but it was still a laugh. "Touché," I said.

"Richard," Chloe said. "Don't be like that." Then, turning to me, "You look tired, Stephen."

"Well, if he is, it's his own fault," Jenny said.

"Been communing with nature again, Stevie-boy?" Somehow Richard's glass was empty again. His eyes had become hooded and sallow.

"Last night's storm," Jenny said.

"I wasn't out for long. It wasn't much of a storm."

"The willow in our front garden would dispute that," Richard said. "I don't understand what you get out of it."

"You wouldn't know," I said. "Not your fault."

"Touché yourself," he said. His smile was small and dark.

*

It started soon after Ben died. Our son was in his first year at Nottingham. He was thriving, by all accounts. He called us often, but not too often. He made friends easily but assured us he was finding time for his studies too and we believed him. We never had a reason not to believe Ben.

The course he chose was Liberal Arts. Jenny was far from happy. She thought it was too woolly, too detached from the real world to be of any practical use. She argued quietly, but persistently, for a more technical choice. Or perhaps he could commit to the Church, become a vicar, as her father had? I remember Ben explaining, typically kindly and gently, that he didn't actually believe in God, so perhaps that route was not appropriate. I remember also our argument later, after Ben had gone; it was understated, of course, but it was intense too, and bitter, and the fault lines that formed then would soon become cavernous and unbridgeable.

It's odd the things that seem important; that can cause loss of sleep and relationships to crumble. But then fate presses its hard, cold hand into your face and you know that these worries carry no weight, are of no importance at all.

A week before he was due to come home for Christmas, Ben attended a party at the house of a friend of a friend. Someone spiked his drink with ecstasy. Just before midnight he said he was feeling ill; he was overheating and finding it difficult to breathe. Someone called an ambulance and they got him to the Queen's Medical Centre on Derby Road within half an hour. It was two in the morning before the police were involved and someone got hold of our number and gave us a call. By then Ben was dead.

*

After they'd gone Jenny started gathering glasses and plates.

"We can do them in the morning," I said.

She put a brandy glass back on the coffee table. "What exactly is wrong with you?"

"What?"

She sat heavily in the chair that Richard had been occupying a few minutes earlier. She stared at the wall opposite. "The sarcasm. The point scoring. Can't we just have a pleasant evening?"

I stood in the doorway that led to the kitchen. Chloe's scent lingered. "I don't like them."

"You seem to like her well enough."

"It's just another phase, though, isn't it, sweetheart? It's been six months, that's longer than usual. I'll give you that."

"I don't know what you mean." She still wouldn't face me. Her back was rigid.

"Kerry and Brian. Terry and Steve. Fiona and David."

"I'm entitled to friends of my own."

"They're not your friends, Jenny."

"What would you know about friends?"

"They're a fad. We were going to go on holiday with Kerry and Brian. Remember? They were round here every week for meals, drinks. Then you dropped them. Just like that. Not very Christian, if you ask me."

"No one's asking you, Stephen." Her voice was small and tight.

I hesitated. When I spoke I tried to load some warmth into my voice. "It doesn't matter, darling. You're getting by, that's what counts. Somehow, we both are."

Her posture stiffened further. However obliquely, I'd touched on the subject of Ben. This had become forbidden territory. I waited. Jenny didn't speak but the atmosphere became hostile, airless. When I could bear it no more I went upstairs to bed.

There was a blizzard on the New Year's Day after Ben died. It hit in mid-afternoon, a vast, relentless wall of snow and sleet. We were in the study, Jenny and I, arranging Ben's funeral. The light through the study window became thin and brittle as the cloud gathered. The radio played low in the corner; weather warnings on repeat. When the snow came we moved to the living room and watched it together wordlessly through the picture window. Jenny eventually spoke in a voice so low that I couldn't hear what she said. She drifted past me and back towards the study. The air did not stir. She carried no scent.

A little later she emitted a single sobbing scream that seemed to come from a part of her that neither of us knew existed. It carried from the study and filled the house with its echo. I didn't go to her; instead I went out of the front door, onto the long, gravelled drive, obscured as it was by fresh, startlingly white snow, and towards the wrought iron gates and the road and fields beyond.

I'm not sure how long I stood there, in the shadow of our house, dressed in jeans and a light sweater, arms spread wide as if to welcome the snow and sleet that drove onto me and into me and caked my face and hair and, perhaps, if I had been able to wait a little longer, would have stopped my heart.

It was George that found me. He was coming to check if we needed anything. He doted on Jenny. He shook me to my senses and pulled me back into the house. Jenny came into the landing when she heard the commotion, then saw the state of me and went back into the study.

George said I needed a hot bath and I agreed. He asked if Jenny was okay and I said that she was, all things considered. He paused at that, unsure what to say. I thanked him and said that I'd be fine, we both would. He left reluctantly, his eyes on the study door.

I had a shower, not a bath; a long one. I thought about the numbing cold, how I'd welcomed it. How small I'd felt at the centre of it all.

Next morning I walked to Vinegar Lake. It's not much of a lake; more a deep, wide pond set against a wall of rock in the centre of our village's long-spent quarry. The water is the colour of vinegar, though. There are a couple of warning signs at the lake's edge, set in the scruffy rubble that runs down to the deceptive shallows that ring its perimeter. The water here is iodine tinted and, in summer, teems with tadpoles and caddisflies and water spiders.

Sometimes the signs are ignored. Most years someone – often young, but not always - will jump into the ugly, acidic water. They don't always come out again.

I stood at the lake's edge and thought about Jenny. Chloe would have been a more pleasant subject; the smell of her, her oddly angled, elliptical smile, but we do not always choose where our minds go. Jenny's grief had driven her further back into her faith and her church. Her father would have been proud; assuming that the bitter old bastard was capable of directing such an emotion at anybody other than himself. He'd always blamed me for Jenny's initial loss of faith, in her teens, at around the time we met at university, all those years ago. But it was nothing to do with me; she was merely growing into herself and away from her timid mother and her father's stifling doctrine.

I was, on the surface at least, deeply cynical and amoral as well as a vocal and committed atheist. It was all a front. I had my own insecurities to hide.

Somehow, Jenny found this combination attractive. I suppose I was passable physically, in those days at least. And I was everything that her father was not. That, to my gratitude and astonishment, was enough. Jenny was a catch. She was deeply pretty in an ethereal and typically English way. And there was money in the family. Everybody said so. Not from the father; vicars weren't rich. But from some distant generation; something shady. Slavery perhaps. I called myself a socialist so the money shouldn't have mattered. But it did, of course.

Once, we were laying on Jenny's bed, in her room on campus, sharing a joint. This brief and mild flirtation with soft drugs was an act of wild rebellion on Jenny's part. I noticed that she barely inhaled, however, and left most of the intake to me.

"I shouldn't be here," she said, gazing at the ceiling, arms splayed loosely above her head.

"I didn't force you."

She gave my head a lazy cuff. "I don't mean that." She took a tiny puff of the joint and passed it back to me. "Dad. He hated the idea of this." She stretched her arms wide, towards the bare, slate-grey walls of her room and the campus beyond. "His precious girl at a common little Uni. The very thought of it."

I shifted on the bed and my hip bumped against hers. A thin patina of blue smoke coated the ceiling. "All part of the appeal, I suppose. You bad girl, you."

"He doesn't really believe that girls need an education. Apart from religious studies."

"Get thee to a nunnery."

"Something like that. Or maybe marry a vicar. Do a little light breeding. Try not to think, though. No good will become of women thinking."

Her voice had become small and bitter. I barely noticed. I was pretty stoned and I'd heard it all before.

I walked the long way home, past the village hall and Jenny's church. Sunlight splashed across the 17th century stonework and the wisteria and the neat, clinical graveyard. I paused at the heavy oak gate. Two young men were working on the guttering to the side of the church's entrance. One was on a ladder, the other stood with his foot on the bottom rung, looking up. They were shirtless and silent. The one on the ground was smoking. The man on the ladder had thick black hair. He looked a little like Ben. They noticed my presence eventually and they turned their heads in my direction. I nodded and walked away. I felt awkward, a little embarrassed. I wasn't sure why.

I walked for another hour or so and saw nobody else; not in the copse or by the wheatfields or in the narrow, sun-flooded streets. Sometimes, living here, I wonder if there has been an apocalypse, some disaster of which I am unaware. More often than not, I find that I don't particularly care if there has.

Back home I realised that Chloe was there before I saw her. Her perfume was heavy in the hallway and kitchen. Jenny's disembodied voice drifted through from the conservatory. There was a sudden pause in the conversation then I heard Jenny say something about houseplants; watering, feeding. Chloe's voice cut in;

lower than Jenny's, the words indistinguishable. Her laughter followed; loud and coarse, drowning out Jenny completely. The timbre of it made something quiver inside me. I am a shallow man. I sometimes wonder if this self-knowledge provides some kind of mitigation. I suspect that it does not.

I reached the conservatory's white-framed doorway. The gaze of both women fixed on me simultaneously. They were sat close together on the long beige sofa, in identical poses; knees together, leant faintly forward, hands linked determinedly in their laps.

"It's you," Jenny said. She sounded affronted.

"I do live here."

Sunlight lapped onto the tiled floor and played itself out into odd shapes across the sofa, the chairs, a tile-topped table.

Chloe said nothing. Like Jenny she wore a sleeveless top. Jenny's was plain navy, Chloe's raspberry coloured and dotted with tiny flowers. The light invading the room seemed to bounce off Chloe. When it hit Jenny it died. It was as though she was absorbing it, holding it greedily within herself. From another room, Jenny's grandfather clock, a family heirloom, struck the hour, ponderous and sardonic.

A little later Chloe made her excuses and left. After another half hour I could no longer bear the stultifying silence so I changed into jogging bottoms and a sweatshirt and said I was going for a run.

I turned left out of our gate and had barely broken out of a brisk walk when I saw Chloe standing by the entrance to a wild meadow; her eyes were fixed on her phone and she was smoking a cigarette. When she saw me she dropped it guiltily to the pavement and ground it out beneath an immaculate kitten heel.

"Busted," I said as I approached her.

"Don't tell Richard. He'd kill me."

"I didn't take you for a smoker."

"Old habits," she said. She closed the screen on her phone and tucked it into her bag. "Very old habits, actually."

There was an odd, small silence. Behind Chloe the meadow was a jumble of ragged, tumbling colour. A pair of Red Admiral's listed drunkenly from flower to flower. The air was sweet and not too hot.

"Were you waiting for me?"

"You wish." Her smile was crooked. Her voice was different from usual; deeper, less mannered.

"This is the first time we've been alone." I wasn't sure why I said that, but it earned a laugh, although it was hard-edged and mocking.

"How romantic." She fetched another cigarette, lit it and took a long pull. "You know my secret now," she said through a long stream of smoke. "No point denying myself."

"My lips are sealed."

"What a sweetheart." She turned to face me. When she spoke again her voice was stripped of all mockery or artifice. "Look, cards on the table, I *was* waiting for you."

"Okay."

"I didn't really see Jenny to get hot tips about caring for my spider plant, useful though that was."

"She certainly knows her houseplants."

"She really does. Talking to Jenny ... it's so ..."

"Frustrating?"

"She's so relentlessly nice." She tapped ash onto the pavement. "Well, to everyone except you, of course."

"Of course."

"She's so bland. So damned soft. So ..." she struggled for the right word, " ...pillowy."

"Pillowy?"

"I think you know what I mean."

"Actually, I do."

"She only ever says precisely what people want to hear. As long as it is not outside her comfort zone. Anything difficult, she just ignores. It's why everyone at the church loves her. She's so warm and lovely. On the face of it. And that's all that matters there, isn't it? Appearances."

"You tell me."

"Not really your thing, is it?"

"You could say that."

"Your absences are noted. Frowned upon."

"Colour me astonished."

She had a tattoo of a butterfly on her left wrist. It was faded, indistinct. She ran a finger across it. The fine hairs on her forearm were silver and erect in the clear light. "Why don't you just come along? For Jenny's sake, if nothing else. It's not as though I believe and Richard certainly doesn't."

"Why bother then?"

"Contacts, dear boy." She shrugged. "And where Richard goes I go."

"Fair enough. What did you want to talk to Jenny about?"

She dropped her cigarette, stamped it out, examined its corpse. "Jesus."

"I would have thought she'd have enjoyed that."

"No. Not ... him." She exhaled firmly and I smelled the nicotine on her breath. "This is difficult," she said. "Can we go somewhere?"

I felt a jolt in the pit of my stomach. "Go somewhere?"

"I feel a bit exposed, standing here like this. This village, you know?"

I did.

I drove to Nottingham on my own the day that Ben died. Jenny couldn't face it. For a while she could barely function at all. A woman from the church stepped in at short notice to look after her. She stayed a week. I remember thinking how kind it was. I haven't seen her since and I can no longer recall her name.

The drive was nightmarish. At the time it seemed endless but now I wonder if it actually happened at all. I suppose it must have because at some point I was required to identify Ben's body. The room they took me to was small and white-tiled and reeked of cleansing fluid. I don't know what building it was in or how I got there. I had intended to visit Ben's room at the University and to speak to some of his friends. I did neither. I found a nondescript B & B where I stayed for three nights. I walked long, pointless loops through an unfamiliar city. It was mid-winter and daylight barely registered; the streetlights were on all day. They cast an appropriately baleful penumbra of sepulchral light. Back in my room I lay on a bed that smelled faintly of semen. I stared up at a water-stained ceiling and thought of Ben's face; cleansed of expression, bone-white, pure, blameless. My thoughts became toxic, boxed in. I barely ate or slept. I was constantly blindsided by the sheer weight of my grief. It seemed demonic, obsessive; intent solely on clinically and systematically hacking away any semblance of light or hope or warmth from my consciousness.

Eventually I drove home. Back in our kitchen, a December evening, rimed with frost, I found my wife and her friend praying to a God in which I could never believe.

We walked eastwards, cutting past the village green to a small copse and a clearing beyond. A couple of tree trunks had been hewn into rough seats. The area was shaded and cool. We sat, closer together than was entirely comfortable. Chloe brushed an imaginary something from the top of her thighs.

"Bugs," she said. "I don't really like this. There's such a thing as *too* much nature."

I shifted on my makeshift seat. "What are you doing here?"

"Sorry?"

I held my arms wide. "Here. This village."

"This fucking village."

"Precisely."

She took a long breath and began to fish in her bag for another cigarette but changed her mind.

"The thing is, we couldn't stay where we were. Things were ... difficult. To be honest, it's become something of a pattern since I've been with Richard."

"I don't understand."

She remained quiet for a moment, her head still, her eyes fixed on a point somewhere past my left shoulder. "Actually ..." she began. She paused again almost instantly. "Look, I'm not Chloe."

"What?"

"And Richard isn't Richard."

"I really don't ..."

"Please," she said, her smile not fitting at all. "Just let me explain."

I raised my hands in mock surrender. "Be my guest," I said. "Fire away."

"We're hustlers, Stephen. Grifters. Richard and I. As good as, anyway."

"I thought you said ..."

"I'm not telling you our real names. It's confusing enough as it is." She moved her head languorously from side to side and smoothed the material of her jeans flat against her thighs. "I can't believe I'm doing this. Trusting you. I barely know you. This isn't me. It isn't me at all."

Instead of asking the same questions myself, like a normal person, I relished the quiet thrill of being taken into the confidence of an attractive woman. "It's not too late, Chloe. You can stop if you like."

"Can I?" Her grey eyes were wide open. Her gaze caught onto mine, reeling me in. "Do you want me to?"

"It's up to you. You can trust me, though." My voice tailed off. It sounded weak, pathetic.

She slid her hand across and squeezed the top of my leg. The skin there tingled long after she'd pulled her fingers away.

"We met in Soho, Richard and I. Years ago. Too many bloody years." This time she did light another cigarette. "I was a waitress." A brief silence. "And a dancer." Another. "An *exotic* dancer, actually. Make of that what you will."

Wordlessly, I did.

"He was good looking, well dressed. Well connected, by all accounts. I was between men, as they say. I thought, why not? I hitched myself to his star, if you'll permit me to mix a metaphor or two."

"You said you're hustlers. I thought Richard dealt in real estate."

"Oh, he does. We do. Have done all over the world. The thing is the land in question doesn't always belong to us. It doesn't always actually exist."

"Christ."

"The trick is to keep moving. Don't get *too* greedy. We've been good at that. So far."

"So that stuff about Richard's father. The inheritance ..."

"All rubbish. A cover story. He *is* a self-made man, though." An arch look, cigarette smoke drifting across her face. "Of sorts."

"You had me fooled. Jenny too."

"Years of practice." She started counting on her fingers. "Richard and Chloe. This is our ... seventh iteration. And probably the last."

"Why?"

She laughed unexpectedly and leant into me. I smelled her scent again and something else underneath. "It's all gone tits up, mate. Richard's fault. He bites off more than he can chew. And he thinks he's being followed. Our past catching up with us. *One* of our pasts. Could be paranoia. He does do a lot of coke." Her shoulder was still pressed against mine. "Poor us, huh?"

"Poor you." I realised suddenly that it had been ages since I'd thought of Ben. I felt drained and empty and ashamed. "Look, I'd better go."

She stood quickly, discarding the cigarette. "Really? Just like that?" She faced me, hands on hips, head tipped to one side. "I'm spilling my guts here and that's all the reaction I get?"

"I'm sorry."

"Sorry? Jesus, Stephen. No wonder your marriage is fucked."

"What? I really don't think ..."

"Oh, come on. You know it. She knows it. The whole world knows it. That house of yours? I mean, it's beautiful, but it's like Ice Station Zebra in there. If it wasn't for her precious God, her *vows*, she'd have dropped you years ago."

I was stunned into silence; both by her choice of words and by the unmistakeable truth of them.

"You want to know what I wanted with Jenny?" She was pacing the clearing, more animated than I had ever known her. "She was a mark, Stephen. I thought she'd be a soft touch. I mean, she's minted right? That house. And there's a holiday home, isn't there? Italy, somewhere like that?" I nodded dumbly. "And she doesn't work. She's very proud of that." She stood still for a moment and looked at me appraisingly. "Where does it come from? The money? I mean, it's inherited, obviously, but the old man was a vicar. There must be more to it than that?"

"I don't know."

"Of course you don't." I tried to say something but she cut me off again. "Thing is, I had a sob story all lined up. Thought she'd be an easy mark. Soft old Jenny. But there's no way in, is there? Not with her." She stood over me, ran her fingers across the top of my scalp. Her voice became gentler. "Well, look who I'm telling."

"Bloody hell, Chloe."

She crouched in front of me and took my hands in hers. "The thing is, Stephen; I'm fucked, you're fucked." She kissed me lightly on the mouth then on the side of my face. "I figured we may as well be fucked together."

The instant that Ben died time broke. It atomised, in the same way that my heart did and my soul. I'm sure that Jenny felt the same and perhaps we could have found some common ground, some comfort, if only we'd been able to talk, to share our experiences like two normal, adult human beings. Instead Jenny hid behind her solid, unyielding God and I found what solace I could by exposing myself to what passed for extreme weather in our part of Norfolk. Not that there was much; the odd hailstorm or downpour or brief, violent storm. I craved a tsunami, a tornado; something localised and brutal and focused entirely on me.

Jenny only said the words once, out loud at least. I mean she thought them, lived them, may as well have had them framed in needlepoint in every room in the house, but she only vocalised them the one time, at breakfast, while she was buttering toast.

"It's your fault." Her voice was light and conversational. She was looking at her toast, which was slightly burnt. "You wanted him to go to Nottingham. You agreed. If he hadn't, he'd still be alive." She took a tiny bite of her breakfast and chewed it slowly. She spared me the merest glance. A millisecond. It burned. It burns still.

Her words were reductive, absurdly so. She was also entirely correct.

When I returned to the house Jenny had gone. I felt lighter than usual, giddy and a little sick. I walked around our home, through its myriad rooms, all spotless, immaculate and shredded with sunlight. It seemed that Chloe's scent was everywhere; in the kitchen, the study and in my bedroom and in the room where Jenny slept. The covers, white and pristine, and the faintly rumpled pillowcase carried no trace of Jenny. It was all Chloe, the sense of her emanating from me, I supposed. It was buried deep inside me; not by love – I wasn't quite that stupid – but by some dreadful, hallucinatory need.

I hesitated by the door to Ben's old room. I ran my fingers along the grain of the stripped pine. I didn't enter.

I took a shower and by the time I'd dressed Jenny was home. We ate dinner together. Pasta with some rich ragu; salad, red wine. It was probably excellent, Jenny's cooking usually was, but I couldn't taste anything.

Jenny was strangely skittish; she had her phone on the table, by the side of her plate and kept glancing at it and touching the screen.

"Expecting someone?"

She shrugged. "Church stuff."

"Hotline to God?"

"Something like that."

After a moment I said, "Have you been with Richard?"

She pushed her phone to one side and appraised me coolly. "Why on earth would you say that?"

"No reason." That, at least, was true. I had no idea where the words had come from.

She took a miniscule sip of Rioja, her eyes still fixed on mine.

The funeral passed, then the autopsy. Misadventure. They never found out who put the drug in Ben's drink; his so-called friends and acquaintances quietly and implacably closed ranks. These were grim, chilly way stations along grief's endless path.

I segued from full time work in a bustling Norwich office to home-working, hours to suit, no pressure, none at all. It was ostensibly very kind of my employer – kitchen design, it's all computerised now – but at our last meeting I could not help but note the relief in my boss's eyes when I confirmed that I would no longer be attending the office. I didn't blame him. Who needed a broken husk of a thing haunting their workplace, pulling everybody down?

I worked fewer and fewer hours. I'm not sure why I bothered at all. Appearances, perhaps. I didn't need the money. *We* didn't need the money. Jenny's family had left her wealthy enough to support both of us without blinking. I suppose I realised deep down – perhaps not so deep, it was pretty bloody obvious – that I needed to keep my options open. Our marriage was as dead and cold as Ben. We both knew this, both knew that the stasis within which we were trapped could not last much longer.

I reached out my left hand and ran my fingers down Chloe's spine. She didn't react. She remained sat up in bed, smoking quietly.

"Well, that's a first for me. I've never cheated before."

"That's a good line," Chloe said.

"It's not a line."

"I'm not quite sure what you expect me to say, Stephen."

"I don't expect you to say anything." I'm not sure that was entirely true. But then again, I wasn't really sure of anything anymore.

We'd met in Norwich for coffee, a couple of days after Chloe had waited for me by the meadow. It was her idea. The café was in a side street near the Guildhall. The day was brutally hot so we found a cool, isolated spot deep in the shop's interior. It was decked out like a library; walls of rich, mahogany shelves crammed with books. We were in an alcove. A ceiling fan churned listlessly above us.

Chloe sat opposite. She placed her sunglasses carefully in front of her. She wore very little; a strappy top and a pair of tiny, lemon-coloured shorts. I couldn't stop looking at her. My son was still dead; would always be dead. My marriage was torn and broken beyond repair. And yet ...

... I couldn't stop looking at her. I knew it was wrong. My self-judgement didn't stop exactly; even then that particular meter was running, still ticking deep in my blood, tucked far enough away that I could only really see Chloe's cool grey eyes and her mouth and the faint sheen of sweat that coated her throat and neck.

A bored looking teenager sporting a nose ring and a tattoo of a blue dragon on her exposed midriff took our order. We both had coffee, despite the heat.

"I've booked us a room," Chloe said, after the girl had gone.

"A room?"

"Yes, Stephen. I assume you are familiar with the concept?" I could see the strain hidden behind the smile. She was trying to sound playful, seductive. I could have told her that she didn't need to work so hard. I was hooked anyway, despite the thread of dark energy that ran behind her eyes and words; despite the fact that I had no real idea of who this woman was. "It's just around the corner. Very discreet."

"Are you a regular?"

There was a flash of real anger then, cutting through the faux-coquettishness but she tamped it down quickly enough. "Funny man."

The girl brought our coffees and dumped them gracelessly on the table. Chloe gave her a smile as well and this one was all over the place. She didn't get one in return and when the girl had left us Chloe braced her arms on the table and stared down at the dark, stained wood. It was as though she was setting herself for something.

"Are you okay?"

"Yes. A little nervous perhaps. Despite your implications I don't tend to make a habit of this."

"I'm sorry." I extended my hand towards hers and she took it. Her skin was cool and dry. "It was a joke. A poor one."

She looked at the coffees in front us. "Look, I don't want these. Shall we go?"

I tried to say something but I didn't want to seem too eager so I just nodded and she squeezed my hand. We both stood and I followed her out onto the baking street.

Ben's funeral was grotesque. It was held at the local church on a bright and severely cold January afternoon. I was outnumbered by people I barely knew. This was Jenny's flock; middle-aged, well groomed, smug amid their obvious affluence and their cosy, unchallenged beliefs. I felt as though I was from a different species. I uttered not a single word of dissent. I let them have their way with me. I was engulfed by their thin, platitudinous sympathy; by their damp, endless handshakes and perfume-drenched hugs.

The vicar said a few words and then Jenny stepped forward. This wasn't planned, not to my knowledge, at least. But I sat in silence and while I listened I burned with shame and a curious flat, cold fury.

Jenny's voice was remarkably clear in the chilled air. She leant against the dais; her face tilted upwards, eyes cast towards her God. I could have been proud of her then, of her unexpected strength and her austere beauty. Perhaps I could have even have loved her again. It was the words that she spoke that were the problem.

Her speech was a paean to God and to her late father. When she mentioned Ben it was not a version of our son that I recognised at all. Her Ben was a devout Christian and had he not been taken so tragically early he would surely have followed in her beloved father's footsteps. There were more words, many more, all devoted to a remoulding of Ben's existence. I looked around at all the pink, adoring faces, glowing in the cold light that angled in through the stained-glass windows.

She glanced at me once, briefly, as she finished speaking. Her face was expressionless but there was a message there and it was for me and for me alone. It said; I win, you lose.

Later, much later, when the whole benighted thing was finally over, a hard, insistent rain fell. I stood out in it for an hour or more. I think I screamed or cried or both. I'm not sure it matters either way. There was no one to hear me.

We did what grownups do. As during the walk to the coffee shop, Chloe led and I followed. Her mouth and hands were soft and warm and eager enough and she appeared to enjoy herself. She also made sure that it didn't take too long. For my part, I didn't do anything obviously wrong and everything worked as it should. This was something of a relief; it had been a while.

When she'd finished her cigarette she lay back again. It was a king size bed so we weren't touching. I glanced at her breasts then looked quickly away.

"It's a little late to be coy, Stephen."

"I suppose it is."

There was sweat on my arms and chest. Her skin was dry.

"I need your help." She was staring at the ceiling. I had a flashback to Jenny and me on her bed at Uni all those years ago. I drove the thought away.

"I don't have my own money. Not much, at least." As I spoke I was calculating; how much did I have? And was it worth it?

"It's not money. Not yet."

"Okay."

She turned on her side. A hand snaked onto my thigh, my stomach, my groin. "I need to get away, Stephen. *We* need to get away." Her voice, which had fallen into a robotic drone, came alive again. She looked into my face. Her lips were slightly parted. I could see the tip of her tongue.

"Just like that?"

"He's gone too far. Richard. He'll be the death of me. Of both of us."

"That's a little bit melodramatic." My voice was not entirely steady. Her fingers worked slowly and skilfully. I thought it would be too soon. It wasn't.

"I know how it sounds." She sat suddenly, releasing her grip. She leant over the side of the bed and fished something out of her handbag. It sat in the palm of her hand. It took a moment to register what it was. A gun. A revolver, I think; small, metallic blue, utterly incongruous.

"Jesus Christ, Chloe."

"A present from Richard. For protection."

"Put it away. Please." I was sat up as well now. My erection had gone.

"It's perfectly safe. I know what I'm doing." She placed it gently back in her bag. "Which is more than I can say for Richard."

I pulled the covers over my waist, as though for protection. "I'm out of my depth."

"You and me both." Her voice was casual now, almost wry. "Things have ... taken a turn. He *is* being followed. Richard. I've seen them. They're driving some big, black thing. Tinted windows. Not very original. It wasn't paranoia. I mean, he *is* paranoid. Richard. You know how he drinks and I mentioned the coke. He really loves that stuff."

"Do you ..."

"Coke? No." She lit a cigarette and folded her arms across her breasts. She seemed comfortable now. Relaxed. She blew smoke away from me. "These are my only vice. Well, apart from fraud, I suppose."

"Where are they from? The guys in the black car?"

"Not sure. London, probably. We were there for a while a few years back. Had an office on the South Bank. We screwed over some pretty shady sorts. I mean, we didn't know they were shady, not until later. But that was a while back and we were careful. Perhaps we weren't careful enough." She tipped ash onto the top of her bedside cabinet. "Maybe it always catches up with you in the end."

"Why don't you just move on? You and Richard? Become ... someone else? Again."

"The money's gone. We're running on fumes. And anyway, I'm sick of him." She moved her shoulder against mine. "Just now, with you? It was nice. You were ... gentle." She could have been talking about a fruit scone, a slice of cake, for all the passion in her voice, but still, I lapped it up. "Richard just takes what he wants."

We'd drawn the blinds, of course. The air was grey and cool. The smoke from her cigarette rose and gathered at the ceiling. "What do you want me to do?"

*

Jenny changed when her dad became ill. They'd been estranged for years, but when Ben was born he softened; he wanted to see his grandson, he said, wanted to be part of his life. He chipped away and Jenny weakened. We were living in a semi-detached in Norwich, happily enough. Her father was in the vicarage, the house we now occupy, just him and a housekeeper, rattling around in far too many rooms.

I didn't think he was ill at first. I thought it was a ploy. Jenny visited frequently; weekends, occasionally for days at a time. She took Ben with her, more often than not. He didn't mind. He was a happy little soul, content to do whatever mummy and daddy wanted. The old man doted on him, by all accounts, although I found it hard to imagine. Still, he didn't infect Ben, at least. Jenny though ... I lost her in increments; it seemed as though she left a little more of herself at the vicarage each time she returned home.

When he finally died – and he took his sweet time, the bitter old bastard – Jenny insisted that we sell up and move to the village. We had the old house stripped and re-modelled. We made it modern and open and full of light. It made no difference; the old man still haunts the darker corners of our house. He haunts the shadows at the end of the garden. He haunts his daughter.

We'd both parked in the multi-storey at St Andrew's. When we reached her car she kissed my mouth and told me to follow her. When I hesitated she kissed me again and said, "Trust me. Please?"

It was ridiculous, of course. But I did.

She drove quickly, cutting corners on the narrow

country roads that led to our village. The drive took half an hour; I had time to think, to weigh up my options. I did neither. My mind kept replaying our time in the hotel room on a fevered, febrile loop. I could still taste her kisses and feel the touch of her fingers on my skin.

Chloe drove to her house, on the outskirts of the village. As she pulled her burgundy hatchback into their wide drive I parked at the road's edge, my engine running. She hurried to my car, impatient, signalling for me to wind the window down.

"Leave it here. It's fine. I need you to come in."

"But Richard ..."

"Richard's not here. You can see that." She smiled to smooth the edge from her voice. It was still stupidly hot. The air was damp and suffocating.

I got out of the car, locked it and followed her into the house.

It was detached, big enough, modern.

"We're renting," she said as she worked the key into the front door. "Overdue, of course."

All the curtains were drawn. The atmosphere was ripe and fetid and dominated by the scent of spoiled food. When we entered the living room she turned the light on. Half-empty takeaway containers crowded the surfaces of a coffee table and large leather sofa. A pyramid of empty beer cans sat next to the large screen TV. There was an overflowing ashtray on the small glass table by the sofa. The glass itself was smeared with a whitish residue.

"Do you like what we've done with the place?" I said nothing. "We tend not to entertain much."

"How do you live like this?"

"We don't settle. I told you."

"You've been here six months."

Her voice hardened. "We're not exactly putting down roots. And stop fucking judging me. Remember what we were doing an hour ago. I was good enough for you then."

"I didn't mean ..."

She came to my side. Her breathing was ragged and irregular. "Who cares about this? It doesn't matter. It isn't real."

"What do you want, Chloe?"

She pressed against me. I could smell her sweat and her breath. "What do you think I want?"

I was trying to formulate a response when I heard the front door open.

Richard's voice. "Chloe?"

"In here, sweetheart." Her eyes were wide open. She looked, briefly, utterly deranged.

"Fuck," I said.

Richard entered the room. He said my name once, then stood very still. Beside me, I was aware of Chloe reaching for her bag.

"Look," I said.

Chloe extended her arm.

Richard's expression changed and he raised both hands to shoulder height.

Before he could speak Chloe shot him twice in the chest.

We reached an impasse of sorts, I suppose, Jenny and I, in the years after Ben's death. All warmth and affection had fled but we kept up appearances, attended some village events together, held dinner parties for Jenny's ever changing cast of church related friends. I played my part, if a little grudgingly at times.

The rules were simple enough; we never touched, we never kissed, we never talked about Ben.

I considered a trip, on my own, of course, to somewhere tropical and wild; to try and find some genuinely extreme weather. I don't think Jenny would have minded. It would have suited her, I think, if I'd simply gone off somewhere and died without fuss. It would have made things easier all round.

I never took the trip. Some crippling, yawning sense of inertia held me back. I made do with minor winds and indifferent squalls.

Perhaps I thought if I stood out for long enough, in the cold, in the rain, that Ben would eventually join me. I'd feel his presence beside me. He'd take my hand.

There was surprisingly little blood.

"I need your help," Chloe said. She tucked the gun back into her bag. She was all business now. She saw the expression on my face. "Come on. We can't leave him here."

He was a big man and death hadn't rendered him particularly helpful. It took both of us to drag him into the hallway. Chloe backed his estate car up to the front door. Somehow we manhandled him into the rear of the vehicle. We had to roll him over the towbar and he ended up face down, arms twisted towards his spine, shirt and trousers askew. At least I could no longer see his face. When we'd finished we were breathing heavily and drenched with sweat.

"Jesus," Chloe said.

I couldn't speak. I was pretty sure I'd put my back out but I was glad of the physical pain as it distracted from the horror show playing on a Technicolor loop in what passed for my mind.

"Where shall we put him?" She looked down on her husband's corpse as though he was an old sofa that needed to be dumped. "Any ideas?"

My brain flooded with an unexpected cold clarity. "Actually, I do." Something in the tone of my voice made her look up. "Do you have anything thing heavy? And some rope?"

There were some breeze blocks in the garage and Chloe found a length of washing line. We loaded them up then I drove my car back to mine and Chloe followed in Richard's. There was no sign of Jenny or her VW Beetle so I parked up and walked back to Richard's car. Chloe was in the passenger seat, checking her phone.

"You can drive. I don't know where we're going." She put the phone between her legs. Her expression was clear and innocent. I did as I was told. I drove us to Vinegar Lake.

The light was beginning to fade and a meaty haunch of cloud was gathering, occluding the sky's eastern edge. It was still as hot as hell.

As I drove my stomach roiled with a sudden cramp. "What the fuck have we done?"

Chloe sucked her lip thoughtfully. "I assume that it if anything happened to Jenny, you'd inherit?"

"What?"

"Just wondering, sweetheart. No need to stress."

I glanced at her as I drove. There was nothing real about her; not in her words, her voice, her expression. I'd sought oblivion in extreme weather and I'd found it instead in the woman next to me. I still didn't know her real name.

*